FAKE MATE FOR THE SOLDIER LION

SPECIAL OPS SHIFTERS

MEG RIPLEY

SHIFTER NATION

Copyright © 2019 by Meg Ripley
www.redlilypublishing.com

All rights reserved. Printed in the United States of America. No part of this book may be used or reproduced in any manner whatsoever without written permission except in the case of brief quotations embodied in critical articles or reviews.

This book is a work of fiction. Names, characters, businesses, organizations, places, events and incidents either are the product of the author's imagination or are used fictitiously. Any resemblance to actual persons, living or dead, events, or locales is entirely coincidental.

Disclaimer

This book is intended for readers age 18 and over. It contains mature situations and language that may be objectionable to some readers.

CONTENTS

**FAKE MATE FOR THE
SOLDIER LION**

Chapter 1	3
Chapter 2	19
Chapter 3	34
Chapter 4	53
Chapter 5	59
Chapter 6	75
Chapter 7	89
Chapter 8	102
Chapter 9	119
Chapter 10	132
Chapter 11	142
Chapter 12	158
Chapter 13	178
Chapter 14	194

FAKE MATE FOR THE SOLDIER LION

SPECIAL OPS SHIFTERS

1

"You feeling okay?"

Leona Kirk tried not to roll her eyes as her brother pulled into the driveway of their parents' house. It was the same question she'd heard about a thousand times since it'd all happened, and she was tired of answering it. The question wasn't really enough to cover everything she felt, and there was no answer that could possibly be sufficient, either. "I'm fine."

Steve shut off the engine but made no move to get out of the car. He turned his deep brown eyes to hers, searching. He had no idea just what it'd been like for her or what it was like for her now, but he was going to push the issue anyway. "Are you sure? I mean, you've been through a lot. Everyone would understand if you don't want to do this."

She flicked her hand impatiently in the air, not wanting him to look at her like that anymore, like she was some sort of invalid. Steve had never been like that. He'd always treated her like the pain-in-the-ass little sister that she was to him, punching her in the arm when she got sassy and teasing her that he was going to throw her in a dumpster. But that was how things were when they were kids, and they definitely weren't kids anymore. Too much had changed.

"I said I'm fine," she snapped, then sighed. "I'm sorry. I'm just testy. This *is* a lot to deal with, but I'm tired of thinking about it constantly. It's hard enough as it is. And getting this little family reunion over with will be a huge load off my shoulders." She opened the car door and swung her legs out. It was difficult not to just bound to her feet, and the pain that still shot up her left calf on occasion served as a continual reminder of everything that had happened in Iraq. Leona blinked back the memories of that terrible day that constantly replayed like a video behind her eyes. Her body would heal, but her mind was something else.

"I'll give you a little warning," Steve said as he came around the passenger side to assist her. "Mom has been a holy mess ever since she got the news. I can't tell you how many times she's called me, fussing and worrying and carrying on."

Leona frowned as she waved away his assistance. She didn't want anyone helping her. She didn't need it, and she sure as hell wasn't going to walk into that house using her big brother as a crutch. "I guess I can't really blame her, given what she must've gone through with Dad."

"Yeah, and that was awful, but you're the baby. She's been desperate to get her arms around you, and it's all I could do to keep her from packing up and flying out to Baghdad herself."

She had to laugh a little at that. Her father had been a military man through-and-through. Nothing fazed him, no matter how crazy or difficult. If there was anything that gave him the slightest bit of worry, it showed as little more than a slight crease between his eyebrows. He'd charge forward and just deal with it, until that last insurrection had dealt with him instead.

Their mother was a completely different person. She had plenty of anxiety, and she didn't hesitate to express it. She'd certainly voiced her opinion when Leona had decided to join the Army. Leona had been somewhat protected from that by all the time she'd spent away from home as she completed one training program after another and advanced through the ranks, finally achieving her dream of becoming a Green Beret. But even then, the letters she'd received from her mother had been full of concern, wondering if she was safe and if she was still certain that military life was for her. Leona could easily imagine how difficult it would've been for those who surrounded her mother when she'd gotten the news that yet another member of her family had been injured in the name of war.

"Now she doesn't have to fly out there. She can see for herself that I'm completely whole and fine." Leona paused at the bottom of the porch steps and looked up at her family home. It was just the same as she remembered it, yet it looked completely different now. The bright red front door framed by white siding and a covered porch were the epitome of American living, especially with the stars-and-stripes flapping noisily in the breeze from the pole her father had installed proudly in the front yard. Some of the flowers in the beds that flanked the porch had been swapped out for different plants, young ones that hadn't yet grown full and bushy. Leona loved the place, but it was like coming home to a dream, something she only vaguely remembered and couldn't be sure she was still a part of.

That red front door burst open before Leona had a chance to think about it any longer. A large woman with her graying hair pulled back in a tight bun shot through the opening and down the stairs far faster than anyone her age should've been able to do, her arms wrapping tightly around her daughter.

"Mom!" Leona said, both choking and laughing. "You're going to suffocate me!"

"Then at least I'd know right where you were!" Mrs. Kirk admonished. "Come on in and sit. Steven, help your sister!"

Her brother gave her a look, and Leona understood. They both knew she didn't really need help, but it would make their mother feel better if they could put on a show. She put a hand on her brother's elbow and went inside, but she was careful not to lean any of her weight on him.

"Hey, there she is!"

"Welcome home, Leona!"

"We missed you!"

Her eyes had barely adjusted to the interior lighting before she was being hugged, kissed, and patted on the back by everyone packed into the living room. Leona could hardly move through the sea of friends, family, and neighbors. She hadn't seen some of them in years, but they were all people she loved. It moved her in a way she hadn't expected, and she was too overwhelmed to do much beyond nodding and smiling. And of course, there were plenty more questions about how she was feeling. These were all answered with her now-standard issue answer of, "I'm fine."

"I tried to warn you," Steve whispered in her ear.

"Just shut up," she said with a forced smile.

The truth was that Leona had dreaded nothing more than coming home. She didn't want the fuss and the mini ticker-tape parade that she knew her mother would insist on. But if nothing else, she was a good and loyal daughter. She would do this and get it done, and then she would go on with her own life.

But there was something both surreal and lovely about seeing so many people she knew and understanding that they cared about her. She quickly blinked to interrupt the beginnings of tears that burned at the backs of her eyes. "This is really great," she managed to murmur.

"Leona!" A pair of slim arms grabbed her from behind.

She patted her sister's shoulder, happy to see that Tracy had been able to make it up from D.C. "Hey, Trace! How are you?"

Her sister held her at arm's length. "Looks like the Army treated you better than the letter indicated. Now we're just going to have to go shopping and do something about those clothes. You look like you've dressed yourself from of Steve's hamper."

"Aw, come on! What's wrong with this?" Leona looked down at the jeans and t-shirt she'd chosen to wear instead of her uniform. It was comfortable and functional, unlike the tailored blouse and pencil skirt her sister wore.

"Tracy, you can bug her about that later. Come sit down, Leona! Steve, get her a pillow!" Her mother had her elbow now, and she guided her to the recliner that had been her father's. "Honey, I've waited far too long to see that beautiful face of yours, and now I want to hear it all from your own lips. Tell us just what happened. Don't leave out a single detail, now. We've got all the time in the world."

Leona sat, but her heart rose up in her throat. She knew this part would be coming. There was no getting out of it. It didn't matter that she'd already recited it all to every doctor and officer who needed it for their paperwork on her way home. It didn't matter that it was the most terrifying thing to ever happen in her life. They wanted to know. It was part of their story now. She knew they would need to hear it, and at least if she recited it now for everyone to hear, she'd only have to do it once.

But as she looked around to see all those expectant faces, her tongue froze to the roof of her mouth. Leona could easily see it all once again right before her eyes. She could give them every tiny gruesome detail, from the almost inaudible click that told her she'd made a life-altering mistake to the deafening roar of the IED as it shoved against gravity. There was even that unmistakable blackness as she'd been thrown several yards away, the ringing in her ears, the way the soldiers around her were hustling with alarm even though Leona hadn't quite figured out what had happened. She'd been stunned and confused, watching the action passively for a long moment while she'd tried to understand what the problem was. After that, of course, was when the pain and shock had begun rippling through her body, torturing her even as the medics rushed to the scene. She could still see their faces, their brows wrinkled as they worked on her.

It was all there, and still just as clear as if it'd happened a moment ago, but she couldn't say it. It was too much. Instead, Leona forced a smile. "Maybe a little later, Mom? I'm pretty tired from my flight."

"Of course, darling! Steve, get her some coffee! Do you want some cake? We got you a beautiful cake." Mrs. Kirk gestured at the coffee table.

Leona recognized the confection as coming from Larry's Cake Castle, the local bakery and her mother's destination for weddings, funerals, baby showers, and birthdays. The frothy buttercream frosting looked disgustingly sweet, and it made her stomach churn, but even that was better than regurgitating all the particulars of her incident. "Is it chocolate?"

"I wouldn't think to order anything else! Steve, cut the cake!" Her mother bustled forward to find the cake knife and fuss over whether the paper plates she'd bought were sturdy enough.

The next half an hour was a blur of noise and happy faces. Leona did her best to appease her mother, knowing just how important this was for her, but it was all too much. It was when she saw her uncle's solemn face at the back of the room, the subtle gesture with his head toward the hallway, that she finally saw her chance for escape.

"Excuse me for just a minute," she murmured as her mother blabbed on to her second cousin about all the medals Leona had earned. She slipped from the chair—with no assistance from Steve this time—and down the hall, spotting her uncle's form just as it disappeared through the door to the study.

She followed him inside and shut the door behind them, grateful for the peace and quiet. She breathed in the scent of her father's study, which had remained unchanged for as long as she could remember. The brown shag carpeting and wood paneling were leftovers from a trend that had died out long ago, but her father had used it to his advantage. He'd filled the room with overstuffed leather furniture, sports and military memorabilia, and even a mounted deer head that his father had killed during a hunting trip.

"Looks like someone's still keeping the liquor cabinet full." Her uncle was rooting around in the solid wood cabinet in the corner behind the heavy oak desk where her father used to sit and pay the bills every month.

"Mom said she does it because she wants to honor his memory, but I think she really just likes to throw back a shot of whiskey every now and then."

She sank down onto the couch, the leather cool against her heated skin.

"Can't say I blame her. Want some?" He rose with a bottle in one hand and his eyebrow arched.

"Damn right I do." She gladly accepted the glass of amber liquid he handed her a moment later, trying to remember the last time she'd taken a drink. "I haven't done this in forever. I didn't want it to interfere with my military ambitions. I guess that's down the drain now."

Her uncle perched on the edge of the desk with his own glass and gave her that same somber look he always had. Like her father, nothing ruffled him. "You taking it all in okay?"

That was at least a different version of what everyone else was constantly asking her, and she knew that her uncle at least partially understood. He'd served ten years before retiring after his older brother's death. "Well, Sarge, that's yet to be seen. I have a lot to figure out, and having a house full of people doesn't make it much easier."

He watched the whiskey in his glass for a moment. "You should be glad this is all it is. Gena was going to rent out the community hall and invite the whole damned town. Your mother thought you deserved a hero's welcome."

"That would've gone over well," Leona sighed as she rubbed the leg that shouldn't be there. It *hadn't* been there just a couple of weeks ago when she'd taken that one wrong step. It was only by taking on her lion form that she'd been able to heal, but of course the general population wouldn't understand how she could've magically grown her leg back. It would've been more than awkward to explain. The new skin was still pink and tender, the bones still figuring out how to support her, but that was a battle that only someone like herself would understand.

"You can't really blame her. You know she was never happy about your dream of following in your father's footsteps. She thought all that was over with, but no. You gave her several more years' worth of sleepless nights." Sarge knocked back his drink and poured himself another.

"And if I had it my way, there would be many more years of them." Leona loved her mother with all her heart, but she wasn't going to let anyone tell her what to do. Except, of course, for the Army. "Hey, don't look at me like that. It's my life, and I was made for the service."

"You going to try to get a desk job?" her uncle asked. "I'm sure there are plenty of them."

Leona sighed and ran one hand through her

hair. She still had her blonde locks pulled tightly back into a low bun. Her honorable discharge meant she could wear it any way she wanted now, but old habits would be hard to break. "Hell no. I can't just sit around. That's not me."

"It never has been," Sarge agreed with a smile. "I remember when I had to get you down from that tree in the back yard. Or when you joined so many after-school activities that you were almost never home for dinner. Or when you wanted to save that old tree at the park—"

"Yeah, yeah. I get it. I've always been a pain in the ass," Leona laughed.

"Yes, but you're one of my favorite pains in the ass," he joked back. "Really, though. What are you going to do now?"

Leona looked down resentfully at her leg. If she'd been human, it wouldn't have been there. The IED would've gotten rid of it, and the doctors would've sewn her up, fitted her with a prosthetic, and sent her home. But she wasn't, and neither was the medic who'd attended to her in the field. He was a shifter as well, and he'd forged her way back home. No one was going to understand how a leg that hadn't been there could suddenly be there again, and so she couldn't do anything but lie about it.

"When I enlisted, I was so excited to be a part of something bigger than myself," she said quietly. "I wanted to make Dad proud. And I can't lie: I wanted those medals, too. I wanted to see new things. Do new things—maybe even things no one else had done before. I had such big plans, but now I don't know what I'm going to do with myself. Anything with the Army is out, and I hate that." She felt the sting of tears again, but this time, they weren't the tears of joy from seeing her family gathered in the living room.

"Yeah, I've been thinking about that. The first thing you need to do is take some time for yourself, Leona. I know that's hard for you, but you deserve it. Take a vacation. Go to the beach or the mountains or wherever suits you. Do what makes you happy without worrying about anyone else. Then, when you're ready to come back, I might have an idea for you."

She felt the spark in her own eyes as she looked up at him, something that she hadn't felt for weeks. "Tell me."

"When you get back," Sarge insisted.

Leona pursed her lips and tipped her head. "Come on! You can't leave me hanging like that. At least give me something to think about while I'm on this *vacation*."

"A vacation you'll never take if you think there's a better option," her uncle pointed out. "All right. Fine. Have you heard of the SOS Force?"

"Can't say that I have."

Sarge put the lid on the whiskey bottle and replaced it in the cabinet. "They're an elite troop of shifters who are called in to handle serious gripes between clans, and they serve the whole country. It's a small force, but all of them are Special Ops."

Her heart and stomach bounced off each other in excitement. "Are you kidding me? That's perfect! How do I get a hold of them?"

Sarge straightened. "I don't know all the details, but I've got a phone number."

"That's fantastic! I'll take it down and go from there." Her skin prickled with anticipation at the thought. A military team that served the shifter community was the perfect place for her. No one there would question her injury.

"I know you'll do great," Sarge agreed, putting his arm around her shoulders as they headed for the door of the study. "And Leona?"

"Yes?" She looked up into his long face. Age had been getting a hold of him. There were wrinkles around his eyes and mouth that she didn't remember seeing there before.

"Your father would be very proud of you."

She pressed her lips together for a moment. "Thanks, Sarge."

2

Hudson rocked back in his desk chair, looking away from his computer and out the window. He hadn't even noticed the hours passing as he'd worked, but that was part of what had made him so successful. When he rested, he rested thoroughly. When he worked, he didn't know how to stop himself.

His company, Taylor Communications, certainly reflected his work ethic. He'd heard all the headlines about it being the fastest-growing tech company on the market, the ratings touting it as one of the best places to work, and the accolades from world leaders about his efforts to spread technology to less developed parts of the world. Those honors reached far past any goals he'd set for himself when he'd first decided to get into the business, but still he knew there was something missing.

But, upon checking his watch, he knew he'd have to think about it another time. He was already late. Hudson rose from his desk and headed out the door. The rest of the floor was already empty, his secretaries and assistants having already left for the day to return to their families. No one was there to see him take the express elevator down to the lobby, hop in his car, and speed across town.

The building that housed the SOS Force's headquarters was much different than his own company's business. A squat concrete building on the edge of Washington, D.C., it could've passed for a small warehouse or maybe an attorney's office. The only thing that really would've given its true identity away was the heavy security in the form of electronic locks that required both retinal scans and fingerprints. He and the others had added a bit of extra protection in the form of a parking garage in the basement so none of their cars would be recognized out in the open.

The other three were already there, their cars in their spots. Even Drake, who'd been in the process of moving, was in attendance. Hudson knew he'd better get his ass into the conference room.

"There you are," Flint said from his seat. His feet were on the table and his fingers were clasped behind his head, looking smug at not being the last to arrive for once.

"I got a little tangled up at work," Hudson said as he grabbed a bottle of water out of the fridge and sat. "I've been working hard on this whole issue of getting cell service to some really remote areas of the Middle East. You know me; I just got started and I didn't stop."

"Yeah, we do know you, but we put up with you anyway," Drake joked.

"I'm surprised to see you here instead of on a screen," Hudson replied. The Special Forces Medical Sergeant was in the process of moving with his young daughter to Eureka, California, where he'd found his mate in the Alpha of a bear clan. "What brings you to town?"

"I've got a few things I still need to button up here before I can really settle down permanently in California," Drake explained. "But the house is pretty much finished, and Lindy has adjusted incredibly well. She's already making tons of friends, but now my sister is talking about joining us out there. That means Lindy won't have a single thing to miss here."

Hudson shifted in his seat. He was happy for his friend, and thanks to the technology provided by his own company, they could have a secure link to chat on no matter the distance between them. But something was making him feel restless. He got up and paced the room slowly.

"I love all the chit chat," Garrison intoned from his end of the table, "but could we get started? Some of us have things to do tonight."

"Another date?" Flint asked with a short laugh.

Before the dragon could reply, Drake cleared his throat. "We got a call earlier today about a clan in Illinois that's having some trouble with an adjoining clan. Apparently—" He was interrupted by a steady beep.

With a sigh, Hudson stood up and strode across the room to a monitor, which displayed the footage from the surveillance cameras he'd installed around the building. Most of the time, the SOS Force never needed them. The building was so nondescript and out of the way that they didn't even get salespeople showing up. It was simply an extra measure, since they didn't exactly want to advertise their whereabouts.

None of the cameras showed anything unusual except the one over the door. Drake, Hudson, Flint, and Garrison always entered through the garage, but there were two regular doors that would serve in case they took public transportation or needed to make a hasty exit. A woman was standing at one of them.

"Looks like we've got some company," he mused, his brow pinching as he studied her face. A far cry from the blurry, black-and-white security footage of the past, she was nearly crystal-clear as she stood waiting at the door. She almost looked familiar, but he couldn't put his finger on her identity. And whoever she was, she clearly thought she was in the right place. "I'll take care of this."

"I can do it so you can get caught up," Garrison volunteered.

"No. It's fine." He was already feeling confined in the conference room anyway, so he headed out into the hall.

Hudson grumbled to himself as he made his way toward the front of the building. He wasn't the type of guy who got anxious. Even while on active duty in the Army, he was always content. They'd had long stretches of sitting around waiting, which he'd passed by mulling over ways to improve the bulky equipment the government insisted on using. And when the shit hit the fan, he simply dove into action and did what he knew how to do best. It was exciting to work with communication and surveillance equipment that allowed him to give the U.S. Army a picture of not just what was happening on a particular street corner, but in an entire country.

It was this thought that made Hudson wonder once again what the hell was wrong with him. He had all the medals he needed to let him know he'd gone a good job while in the service. He'd taken advantage of his G.I. Bill and gone to school, excelling in his technology and business classes. Even once he and the others had started up the SOS Force, he'd still found the time to continue to grow his company, which had started out as little more than a dream and caffeine-fueled nights of ideas. He had everything a man could want.

He'd have to deal with his existential problems later, though. Hudson reached the front door and pushed a small button to the side. "What can I do for you?" It was the most generic question he could ask without giving anything away about what actually happened there.

The woman looked straight into the camera with confidence. "I'm here to apply for a job," she said evenly.

"I'm sorry. I think you have the wrong place." He

let go of the button and watched the monitor, expecting her to walk away.

But she remained exactly where she was. "No, I don't. This is where I'm supposed to be. It took a little time to find you, but I did."

He tipped his head to the side, studying her through the screen. She couldn't see him, and he had the advantage, but her confidence was throwing him off. He pushed the button again. "We're not hiring at the moment."

She nodded as though she expected this. "That's just because you don't know what you're missing yet. But I think the SOS Force could use me."

Hudson's heart froze for a moment. The conclaves situated around the country all knew about the SOS Force. They couldn't be a complete secret, or else no one would ever be able to come to them for help. But for someone to stand right there on the doorstep and announce who they were wasn't something he was comfortable with. He flicked the locks and opened the door.

Even that quick action didn't startle her. She looked at him with that same calm visage he'd seen on the monitor, as though she'd been looking at him the entire time. She even gave him a small smile. "Sergeant Leona Kirk, U.S. Army Special Forces."

She offered him no salute or handshake, still just standing as calmly as ever on the doorstep.

His throat tightened. Hudson felt a twitch at the end of his spine and a tingling on his neck, and he fought the lion inside him that was suddenly so desperate to shift. He had no idea who this woman was, but she was definitely affecting him. He pressed his tongue against the tip of a tooth that was slowly sharpening itself to a point.

Hudson glanced around, checking the street outside for any sign of foul play. No one had ever just come up to their building like that, not even someone who was lost and looking for directions. Something had to be off here. The first thing he could do about it was get this woman off the street so he could figure it all out. He held the door open a little wider. "Come in."

She did so without hesitation, but Hudson noticed that she quickly took in her surroundings. She was still completely relaxed—at least as far as he could tell—but she was behaving the way anyone who'd been training to head into dangerous territories would. You never let your enemies—or potential enemies—know when you were bothered or by what. And of course, if she really was with the Special Forces, then heading into a plain concrete building in the nation's capital was pretty tame compared to anything else she'd done.

He shut the door behind her. "Would you care to tell me what you're doing here?"

Those deep brown eyes met his, and Hudson's stomach turned to liquid. "I already told you. I'm looking for a job."

"And just what sort of job do you think you'll get here?" Damn it. This woman was creating the kind of reaction in him that he'd always heard about but never actually experienced. Finding a fated mate was the kind of thing shifters of all kinds spoke of, and he knew from Drake and others that he was close to that it did really happen. But when you hadn't experienced it yourself, it didn't quite seem real. Whoever this woman was, she was proving him wrong without doing anything but showing up.

"Hopefully one that's challenging, engaging, and exciting," came her simple reply.

He studied her face, though he was peripherally aware of her entire body. Her blonde hair shimmered with a myriad of gold even under the LED light fixtures. She had it drawn back tightly from her face, but that only served to highlight her astounding cheekbones. The woman was muscular, her strength evident even in her modest clothing of a simple V-neck t-shirt and jeans, but she retained the curves of her gender. He swallowed as yet another shiver of energy rippled over his skin. "As I said, we're not hiring."

"I understand," she replied. "And I even understand why you're not willing to admit who you really are. But any place that has this much security has to be housing something pretty important. Maybe it would be better if I just let you have this." She reached into her pocket.

He was ready, just in case she wasn't who she said she was, but he didn't need to worry. Sergeant Kirk simply pulled out a familiar piece of paper that he recognized as a DD-214. Hudson took the paper from her and glanced it over, noting her separation designator. "You were injured?" She definitely didn't *look* injured.

A slight dip of her head acknowledged this, but she didn't offer to go into any details.

That, at least, Hudson could understand. He'd been one of the lucky ones, getting out of the Army simply because he was ready to pursue his own life instead of being forced out by a life-changing injury. Shifters healed fairly quickly if they had the opportunity, but that didn't mean it would be any easier on them. Nothing was easier for a shifter when they had to deal with humans who didn't understand. "And what makes you so confident you should be here?" It would be so much easier to just dismiss her and send her out the door, but a part of him didn't want to let her out of his sight ever again.

"I've heard a little about what the SOS Force does and was given your address by someone in the know. As you can see, I've got an honorable discharge for my injury, but I can't just stop. I'm not going to get a job as a pencil pusher and be happy. I think you could use me, and I could use you." She kept her gaze solidly on him.

She had no idea how much those words were getting to him. But he was trained, just as she was, and he could keep his cool as long as he needed to. Hudson lifted the paper slightly as he spoke. "I'll keep this on hand, but I can't promise anything. And of course you know that even a paper that looks this official doesn't mean anything until we have you thoroughly and officially vetted."

Sergeant Kirk showed her first sign of irritation in the way she lifted her chin, but she quickly regained her composure. "I understand. I took the liberty of writing my phone number on there. Feel free to call me when you're ready." She turned on her heel toward the door.

Hudson strode forward to open it for her and she left without turning around to look at him or saying anything further. He watched her go until she reached the street and turned down the sidewalk.

He closed the door behind him and leaned against it for a moment. Surely, that didn't just happen. But it most definitely had, and no matter how much the logical part of him wanted to deny it, he had a lion inside him that was fighting madly to get out and follow that woman. She was intoxicating, from the way she looked to the way she sounded. He'd wanted to shift, to show her his true form, maybe even to sink his sharp teeth just far enough into her neck to let her know what he thought about her. But she was gone, and this wasn't the way he was supposed to be thinking when he was on the job. He launched himself off the door, made sure it was locked, and headed back to the conference room.

"You finally done flirting?" Flint cracked when Hudson came back into the room.

Hudson shot him a glare. The Special Forces Weapons Sergeant had hit too close to home, even though Hudson had done his best not to show Kirk any signs of what she'd done to him. "Believe it or not, asshole, she knew exactly who we were and wanted to work with us."

The other men stared at him in shock for a moment. "You're shitting me, right?" Garrison asked, leaning forward with his elbows on the table.

"I'm afraid not. She's a Green Beret, honorably discharged from the service for an injury she wouldn't discuss. But she basically left her DD-214 as a resume, and if it's accurate, then she's one hell of a soldier."

"Let me see." Drake took the form, giving a low whistle as he looked it over. "That's quite a record, and it looks like she's got plenty of chest candy."

Hudson felt his face flush at the mention of medals, even though he knew it had nothing to do with Sergeant Kirk's stature. "Yeah, and she's good enough that she knew exactly who we were and where we were. Hell, she probably even knows my name." The thought of his name coming from that woman's lips distracted him for a moment.

"A new team member might be just what we need," Garrison mused. "It's been just the four of us all this time. She might bring something new to the table."

"Wouldn't hurt to have some extra backup now

that Drake is gonna be off fucking around in California," Flint cracked.

"Such a comedian," the doctor muttered. "I hate to say this, but since we're talking about letting a woman join, we'd have to be careful. None of us could get involved with her. I wouldn't want something like that to interfere with our work."

"No, of course not." All the men agreed, even Hudson, but he knew that wasn't going to be easy for him. He'd already stood close to her, felt the way his body reacted to her presence. He pinched his wrist under the table to get himself back to the matter at hand. "But we can worry about all that later. You said we had a call come in?"

Drake set the strange woman's discharge papers aside. "Yes. There's a pride in Illinois that claims a neighboring pride is involved in some illegal weapons. They're selling guns and knives to anyone who comes to them with the right price. That activity is leaking onto the secondary pride's territory, which is why they called us."

"I could see why that would be a problem for them, but it just sounds like a day in the park to me," Flint replied with a slow smile. "I wouldn't mind a chance to rifle through their inventory. I'll go."

Drake put out a hand to defer him. "I'm sure you

would, but this particular part of the country happens to be thick with lions. I don't think your wolf would fit in all that well."

Flint threw his hands in the air in frustration. "You're no fun."

"No, but you knew that. What do you say, Hudson?" He turned to the Special Forces Communication Sergeant. "Think you can pull this off?"

A distraction from that unexpected woman at the door was exactly what he needed. "Absolutely. Let's get some more information. You got the recording of the call?"

3

Leona stared blankly at the television. She'd hardly seen anything that had come across it in the half-hour since her sister had been home. All day, she'd looked forward to Tracy getting home from work just so she had someone to talk to. Being cooped up in the apartment was driving her crazy. "I don't know how you watch this shit," she finally said, propelling herself up off the couch. "All these reporters are just sitting in a studio, covered in hairspray and makeup, pretending they know what the hell they're talking about."

Tracy looked up at her, startled. "I can change it. We don't have to watch the news. I can put Netflix on, or a movie or something."

"No, it doesn't matter," Leona said with a sigh.

"I'm sorry. You've been nice enough to let me stay here, and I've been a shitty house guest. It's just really hard to sit still when I've spent almost the last decade of my life constantly on the move, constantly learning and training, constantly preparing for the next battle." She went to the window, seeing the same scenery she'd already memorized. The red car that had been parked at the house at the corner was now gone, and a couple of children played in a sprinkler at another house, but otherwise nothing had changed.

"Yes, I've noticed."

"What's that supposed to mean?" Leona rounded on her sister.

"That you're restless," Tracy explained simply. "You're not meant for suburban life, but I don't think that would come as a surprise to any of us. I remember when you used to go to Girl Scout camp as a kid. You'd get out there, canoeing across the lake, hiking through the woods, exploring and adventuring. You never wanted to come home when Mom came to pick you up, and if I remember correctly, you even tried to run away once so you wouldn't have to leave camp."

"True enough." Leona remembered those days well. It was one of the few times in her life when she felt as though she could let her true nature show, even if she wasn't able to shift into her other form. Her father had always been proud to hear about her adventures, and Leona knew that had only encouraged her to keep going.

"I have a feeling you were the same way overseas. You were out there on some campaign, and you weren't ready to come home. You're pacing the place like this is some fortress you're trapped in, and you expect the enemy to come rushing up any moment." Tracy clicked off the TV and sat forward in her chair. "I'm not sure it's healthy."

Her sister's comment darkened Leona's already bleak outlook. "I love you, Trace, but don't bother talking to me like you have any idea what I've been going through. You said yourself that I'm not made for this life."

"Well, maybe I spoke too soon." Tracy stood, still dressed in the pale cream skirt suit she'd worn to the office. "I know you've always chosen to express the—shall we say—wilder side of yourself, but there are plenty of other places in the world for a lion. I mean, look at me. I've climbed the corporate ladder with such ferocity that *Working Mother* wrote an article about me. It doesn't all have to be quests and escapades."

Leona closed her eyes for a moment, trying to keep her patience in check. Just like their animal counterparts in the wild, the lion shifters were a close family. They depended on each other for safety and comfort, and even when they had their differences, their spats never lasted for long. Even so, Leona wasn't sure her sister would ever truly understand. "I don't think the concrete jungle is the place for me. But you don't have to worry about me wearing tracks in your carpet. I've got a lead on a military-related job I'm working on. I just have to wait and see what happens with it."

"Care to tell me what it is?"

"Not really, to be honest." The idea of getting accepted (or rejected) by the SOS Force was weighing heavily enough on Leona's mind, and she didn't need her sister to bring all her own arguments to the table.

This, at least, Tracy could accept. "I'm here if you need me. And I'm sure with your service record, you won't have a problem. While you're waiting, why don't you come in here with me and we'll get some dinner made?"

Leona followed her into the kitchen and washed her hands, but her mind wasn't on food. She was thinking instead about the way her body had vibrated as she'd approached that strange, squat building that housed the SOS Force. It hadn't looked like much, and while she had been around long enough to know that a team like the Force wouldn't just put up a neon sign, she'd had her doubts. But then she'd seen the security camera that swung around a little too quickly to focus on her. It wasn't a model she was familiar with, and it definitely wasn't part of the typical security systems people bought at the computer store. She'd also noted the electronic locks on the door, which also weren't the norm. They looked more like something out of a movie, and that was all the indication Leona had needed to know she was in the right place.

And then there had been *him*. He hadn't given her his name, but she didn't need it in order to have him stick in her mind. He was hot, with dark blonde hair that he kept swept back from his face. He was tall and broad, and Leona had sensed the powerful muscles just beneath the surface of his skin.

Though she'd spent the last several years focusing on her career instead of men, Leona wasn't the type to just ignore a good-looking guy. She wasn't immune. But there was something much more intriguing about that man than simply the way he looked. His amber eyes had penetrated straight into hers and down to her soul. She could tell they were breathing the same air as they studied each other, and Leona had felt the distinct urge to slip out of her human skin and show him her more feral side. She'd needed him, right there in that little lobby area he'd allowed her into, in a way that made her want to lick his skin right where his heart beat at his throat and run her hands over the hard planes of his abs.

Which was ridiculous, of course. Now that she wasn't anywhere near him, she wanted to be more rational about the whole thing. She couldn't just tumble over herself for a strange guy, except that she had. As focused as she'd been on finding a new career, she couldn't stop thinking about him ever since she'd left.

"Hello?" Tracy's harsh voice cut into her fantasies about the man. "Are you listening to a word I'm saying?"

Leona blinked. Damn. She wasn't the kind to just space off like that. She was always paying attention, always listening, always ready. That was the kind of training she'd received in order to become part of the Special Forces, and it'd become second nature over the years. How strange that she could drop it so suddenly for someone she was...No. Even in her mind, she didn't want to admit the words that described that encounter. "Sorry. I was thinking."

"Clearly," Tracy replied with a snort as she took a package of steaks out of the fridge. "What I was trying to say is that you should have a backup plan."

"What?" Leona's mouth focused on the bloody meat. Tracy must have purchased it recently, and from a butcher who actually kept his product clean and fresh. She hadn't realized until that moment just how hungry she was.

Her sister sighed impatiently as she lit the flame under a cast iron pan and sprinkled it liberally with olive oil. "I'm trying to help you. The least you could do is listen."

The last thing Leona needed was for her sister to chastise her, but that had always been Tracy's way. She'd taken her role very seriously, even when they were little, constantly snatching at opportunities to boss Leona around or get her into trouble. As they'd gotten older, Tracy always wanted to share her advice about men and careers, even when Leona had made it clear she wasn't interested. She had her own life and her own decisions to make.

Now, she felt much the same way. Tracy only had a couple of years on her, and she wasn't the one who'd been off to war. She hadn't seen people starving in their own villages. She hadn't seen the kind of death and destruction that conflict caused, eating away at everything in its path. She'd lived an insulated life in a safe place where the biggest worry she'd had to deal with was a traffic jam on her way home from work.

Still, Leona loved her sister, and she did appreciate Tracy letting her stay at her place when she'd suddenly found herself without her military brethren around her. She was right. The least she could do was listen. "Okay. I'm paying attention this time." She took a head of lettuce out of the fridge and began tearing it apart to make a salad.

"I've been thinking a lot about you since the news about your injury reached us," Tracy began. "We were devastated, even once we knew you'd be all right. But anyway, that's not really what I want to talk to you about. I mean, you're getting around just fine."

"Yeah, mostly." Leona glanced down at that leg that wasn't supposed to be there. It was almost unfair that she should be fine when there were so many other soldiers who weren't. Shifter or not, every man and woman over there was fighting for a cause bigger than themselves, and yet many of them lost part of themselves. It happened physically or mentally, or both.

"What I'm trying to get at is that you always envisioned the Army would be your entire career. I remember when you told us officially that you were enlisting. There wasn't a single thing anyone could say to sway you. That was the only thing you were interested in. But now you can't do that anymore, and you didn't have a backup plan. Maybe this job you're hoping to get won't work out either, and you should have a backup plan for it as well."

"Who's to say I don't?" Leona tore at the lettuce, tempted to whip out her claws and shred it properly, feeling slightly offended.

"Do you?" Tracy challenged as the sound of sizzling meat served as a backdrop for their conversation.

Leona growled softly. "No." The SOS Force was the only thing she'd concentrated on ever since Sarge had told her about it.

"Okay, so here's an idea. Maybe think about settling down. Acclimate yourself with the local pride. Get a nice little house with enough space for a garden. You could get all sorts of jobs with your background, something without too much of a commute."

"That sounds like an absolute nightmare." She'd said the words harshly, but as soon as they were out, Leona began to laugh. Tracy wanted the best for her and was concerned for her, but the two of them were always at such odds with each other.

"What? Why?"

But Leona didn't have a chance to answer. Her phone had suddenly started ringing in her pocket. She didn't recognize the number. "Hello?"

"Sergeant Kirk, this is Hudson from the SOS Force."

Oh, yes. She knew exactly who he was as soon as he said her name, and a shiver of excitement rippled down Leona's spine and coalesced in her stomach. She now knew the name of the man who'd been haunting her mind for the last day and a half, the man she hadn't been able to stop thinking about. But this wasn't the time for that sort of stuff. She slipped out of the kitchen and down the hall. "Yes, this is Sergeant Kirk."

"I need you down here in five minutes for a meeting."

It was completely out of the blue. It wasn't even reasonable. But that didn't bother Leona. It was probably a test, and she was more than ready to pass it. "I'll be right there."

Her knuckles itched as she hopped out of the cab a block away from headquarters. Her body was full of energy, and she could almost see it flashing brightly through her veins. It took everything not to shift, to feel her paw pads against the sidewalk as she raced toward this new destiny.

Retaining her self-control and her human form, she stepped up to the door and rang the bell.

Hudson appeared instantly, whipping the door open. His jaw was tight and his eyes intense, almost as though he was angry with her for being there. "Sergeant Kirk. Come in."

She did as she was told, taking care to keep her shoulders straight and her head up. How easy it would be to rub her hip against his as she slipped in the door, to rub her jaw against his shoulder as she looked up into his eyes, to tell him what he did to her. Her abdomen tightened as she fought it all off. "I hope I didn't keep you waiting."

He didn't even glance at his watch. "You're right on time. The conference room is this way." Now it was his turn to move past her.

Leona had to wonder if he was feeling the same way. She'd never suspected anyone of being her fated before. She knew it had to be a mutual thing. A pull this strong couldn't simply be a one-sided thing, yet he seemed just as solid and steady on the surface as she was fighting to be. She said nothing as she followed him down a hallway to a conference room with massive windows and an equally large table.

"This is Flint, our weapons specialist," Hudson said, indicating a man who lounged back in his chair and picked his teeth with a pocket knife. "Garrison, our engineer." He gestured toward a man who sat with his back straight and his eyes watchful, but accepting. "Our resident physician, Drake."

This last man was seated at the head of the table, and he stood up to shake her hand. "It's nice to meet you, Sergeant Kirk. We think you might be a good fit for the SOS Force, even though Hudson wasn't kidding when he said we weren't hiring."

That was more of a compliment than she would've expected from men like this. "I appreciate the chance."

"And it'll be an interesting chance," Garrison intoned from the other end of the table. "We've received some information, and there's a pride in Illinois we need to investigate. We don't do these things overtly, preferring to keep our presence quiet until it's time to take final action. We've discussed this quite a bit since you arrived, and we've decided to send you and Hudson on the mission."

Her heart thundered with excitement. It hadn't been all that long since she'd been hurt, but the intervening time had seemed like an eternity. There was nothing she wanted more than to get back out in the field. On the backside of that thought came the immediate awareness of Hudson, standing just behind her. So she was going to be his partner on this assignment? She wasn't sure how she felt about that. "I'm more than happy to go out on my own."

Drake gave her a small smile. "I have no doubt about that, considering your service record, but considering you're brand-new to our team, we're not inclined to send you out alone. You'll be heading into a suburban area, and you and Hudson will pose as mates to blend in."

"I see." Those were the only words she could choke out, considering how every cell in her body was thrashing toward Hudson at that very moment. She couldn't deny the attraction she felt for him, and now they were assigned partners? Pretend mates, even? It was like torture, and it was going to make this mission much harder than any of them could know. "When do we leave?"

The grunt of laughter came from Flint, who was

now twirling his knife expertly with his fingers. "There are some things we need to do first. You can't just head out without knowing what you're going into, and you've got to have a link with the rest of us."

Leona had expected to spend some time learning about this mission, but this caught her off-guard. "A link?"

"Just like a clan," Hudson said from behind her shoulder.

She stepped away to look up at him, acutely aware of how little distance there was between the two of them.

"My company has provided the Force with special phones and secure lines to communicate from anywhere in the world, but of course that doesn't work as well when we're in our other forms. We forge a mental link to each other just like any other clan does." His eyes slipped down to her mouth for only a split-second before returning to her eyes.

She swallowed, the idea of Hudson being in her mind both thrilling and terrifying to her. "And how do we do that?"

"A sacred ritual," Garrison replied. "Knowledge of this ceremony has been passed down through my family for centuries, even when there was no need to use it. I tried it when the four of us teamed up, and it was just what we needed. I assume you're not afraid of blood?"

"Doesn't bother me at all." She'd seen plenty of it, both her own and others'.

"Good. We'll go over all the information for the mission right now, and then we'll conduct the ceremony tonight. We leave in the morning." Hudson gestured for her to sit down before taking the chair next to her.

THE FIELD WAS A REMOTE ONE, and Leona might never have found it if she hadn't had such thorough land nav skills drilled into her brain. She'd wondered as she drove if this was just some trick by the SOS Force, some hazing that was supposed to embarrass her and let her know she wasn't truly welcome in their group. But there she stood with the four men in a clearing surrounded on all sides by woods, a ring of stones filled with firewood in the center. No fire had been lit, and only the dim blue light from the stars and the sliver of moon overhead illuminated the field.

Hudson watched her as she joined them, but it

was Garrison who spoke. "This is a relatively simple ceremony, but you must understand that it's not only extremely important to the SOS Force, but to my people as well. We no longer dabble in magic as our ancestors did, but if word of what's about to happen here were to leave this circle of people, there would be consequences."

"I understand." Leona had no interest in outing these men to the rest of the world. She needed them if they were truly going to provide her with the type of lifestyle she craved so badly.

"Good. Flint?" Garrison looked to the weapons specialist.

Flint pulled a slim knife with a curved blade from a sheath at the back of his belt. It glinted even in the starlight as he hefted it in his palm. "They just don't make them like this anymore. I want to borrow this from you sometime, Gar. I need to try my hand at replicating it."

"Unless you can find a dragon willing to sacrifice his claw for the handle, you're out of luck." Garrison took the knife from him and looked back at Leona. "The first task is for each of us to make a small cut, one on each forearm, big enough to flow but not so much that it'll kill you." He grinned as he used the knife to easily slash the thin skin just above his wrists and then pass the weapon to Drake.

Leona was last, and by the time she received the knife, it was already dark with blood. The handle was curved in the opposite direction of the blade, smooth and conical, made of a dragon's claw as Garrison had indicated. She didn't hesitate, knowing they were watching, and made the required lines before handing the knife back to Garrison.

He nodded as he accepted it. "And now, we shift." Garrison was already transforming as he spoke, his shoulders rolling as massive wings unfurled from his back and formed a silhouette against the stars.

Leona didn't make a habit of shifting in front of strangers. She felt her cheeks burn slightly as her spine elongated and her tail swished in the darkness. Her fingers thickened and shortened as her palms became tough and dark. A short coat of gleaming gold fur erupted all over her body, and she felt the familiar pain of her face changing into a muzzle. Soon enough, she stood in the field not with four men but with a dragon, a bear, a wolf, and a lion. Garrison puffed up his reptilian chest and sent out a stream of flame that ignited the wood in the center of the clearing with ease.

Leona couldn't help looking up at Hudson who

stood proudly next to her in his animal form. His mane was gloriously long and thick, dark against the paler fur on the rest of his body. He returned the gaze, the fire flickering in his eyes. Her true form had been demanding to come out, but now that it had, Leona didn't know how well she'd be able to control it. He still had that power over her, that power that made her stomach twist into knots.

"Your wounds must touch, so that the blood flows through each of us." Garrison's voice had changed now that he spoke with such a long tongue and sharp teeth.

They did as they were told. Leona reached out with her right paw so that her leg crossed that of the dragon's and their lacerations touched. She felt the heat of Hudson on her left as he did the same, and a spark jolted through her as soon as their bloodstreams coalesced. She pressed her tongue against the back of her teeth to keep from gasping.

Garrison was speaking now in a rasping language that she didn't understand. His eyes were closed, the fire dancing on his emerald scales, and it was as though they were the only creatures in the universe. He then repeated the words, translating them into English. "Our blood becomes one, flowing within each other. Bonded as brothers, our nexus strong."

A ripple of energy shot up Leona's left arm, across her chest, and down her right arm. It pulsed and throbbed, repeating until she wondered if she was having a heart attack. Her limbs grew weak between the surges, but she felt new strength flowing into her as they returned. Then they were gone altogether, and when Garrison withdrew his arm slowly from hers, she felt a distinct chill in his absence. Hudson did the same, breaking the circuit on that side, and the coldness he left was almost enough to send her to her knees.

It is done, the dragon intoned.

It took Leona a moment to realize that he'd spoken inside her head. *That was it?* It seemed like such a simple rite.

I admit some of the meaning is lost in translation. She could hear Garrison's laugh inside her head as easily as her words.

You all right? This was from Drake, his bear eyes a shade darker than the thick fur of his face.

Yeah. I think so.

Good. Like I said, we leave in the morning. Hudson turned and left the circle, his tail swishing as he melted into the woods.

4

Hudson flicked his finger across the touchscreen of his computer, checking that everything urgent was taken care of before he left town. He had very capable people working for him, and he knew he could rely on them to make the right decisions in his absence, but he didn't believe in leaving any more work for them to handle than was absolutely necessary. He would do better on this mission if he knew Taylor Communications was taken care of.

He'd left early in the afternoon that day to make sure he was at headquarters on time. He and the guys needed to make sure they were in concurrence about the mission, and Hudson wanted to come back to the office to make sure everything was buttoned up before he left.

And hell, what kind of mission would it be? Pretending to be the mate of a woman who drove him absolutely crazy? He could see the stubbornness in Leona's eyes, her willfulness. She was clearly the type of woman who was used to being independent. Hudson was a successful man who was well-known. There were plenty of women who fawned over him, wanting him to take them out on elaborate dates. He was used to being the one in charge when it came to relationships, but Sergeant Kirk wasn't going to just fall at his feet.

And seeing her as a lioness? That had nearly undone him. Even with only the firelight, Hudson could see just how glorious she was. Her coat was the color of caramelized butter, with a few darker lines that dripped down her back and between her ears. Her muscles were sleek and strong under that fur, her muzzle proud and her ears attentive.

That had been difficult enough, but then he'd actually touched her. Hudson faced his computer screen, but he didn't actually see what was in front of him. He could only see the side of Sergeant Kirk's face as his arm had touched hers, the way her ear had twitched as that electrical spark ignited between them. It was unlike anything he'd ever experienced before. Even the first time he'd done that ritual with Garrison, Drake, and Flint, there had only been the subsequent pulses of energy once the words were spoken. There was definitely something going on between himself and Leona.

Of course, now she was part of the Force. Hudson had agreed immediately that none of them should get involved with her. Should he have admitted they were fated? The idea had seemed so strange, but he'd known it was true.

The gentle knock on his door made him refocus his eyes, and he blinked in the light of the screen. Looking up, he found Drake standing in his doorway. "Hey, what are you doing here? It's late."

The doctor smiled. "I know. That's exactly why I came to check on you. You seemed a little…off today. When I drove by and saw that you'd left all the lights on, I thought we might need to have a little chat."

Hudson knew that Drake's visit couldn't be completely innocent. His office was out of the way, and his friend would've had to have come here on purpose. "I'm fine. Just one of those days."

"If you say so. I guess I wanted to make sure it didn't have anything to do with me moving to California. I know we all settled in this area, thinking it would be a good way to still live our own lives while being able to have a centralized headquarters." Drake lowered himself into the chair in front of Hudson's desk, looking solemn.

Hudson was grateful for the chance to turn his thoughts away from his own concerns. He felt warm appreciation for his friend. They'd served together, both while enlisted and while discharged, and that had created just as much of a bond between them as Garrison's ancient ceremony had. "No, man. Nothing like that. We never made a pact to live within a mile radius of each other or anything, and if nothing else, your move has pushed me to advance some technology I might've set to the side otherwise. You've found something really good in Nikita; you can't just deny that."

Drake smiled at the mention of his mate. She was a gorgeous blonde, and all the guys knew just how smitten the two of them were. "You're right. She's really something else. Lindy's crazy about her, too. And that's all I really need to know that I made the right decision."

"You did." Hudson glanced at his computer screen again. The next item on the To Do list from his secretary was a missed phone call that afternoon from Belinda Cates. An executive with a small finance company, the two of them had shared a business lunch the week before. Apparently, she was wanting to have dinner with him sometime soon. He couldn't make himself feel flattered, knowing from just the short time he'd spent with her that she was only looking for money and status. Hudson swiped the message to the side.

"If you have a moment, I wouldn't mind talking about Sergeant Kirk," Drake said, shifting a little in his seat. "I have a few doubts."

"I can understand that," Hudson replied slowly. He was having plenty of his own doubts, but probably not for the same reasons.

Drake leaned his elbows against the arms of the chair and crossed one ankle over his knee. "I think we need to keep an eye on Kirk."

Hudson lifted his brow. "I'm a little surprised to hear you say that, if I'm honest. You seemed all for her joining."

The doctor nodded. "I was, and I still am. As the others said, she might have a lot to contribute. But we've been such a small team all this time, and I worry that we might've made the wrong decision."

It was difficult to envision Kirk as anything other than what she'd presented to them: a wounded veteran looking for a way to continue the life path she'd started. *And fucking hot.*

"I'm just asking you to keep an eye on her, that's all. Don't let her try to complete this mission alone. We have no reason to mistrust her, but neither do we have any reason to just hand over the reins. Does that make sense?"

"Of course. I'm sure it'll be fine." Hudson forced a smile. "Any other last-minute advice?"

Drake rose from his seat. "Just be careful. I'll be in touch." He walked out, leaving Hudson to contemplate just what he was getting himself into.

5

Leona glanced around as Hudson glided the rented vehicle through the suburbs of Edwardsville, Illinois. It was a mix of historic-looking brick buildings and modern constructions. The streets were busy but clean, and the sun shone too brightly on all of it. "Are you sure we're in the right place?"

Hudson glanced at her from the driver's seat, dressed in a pale blue polo and jeans. Somehow, he looked completely relaxed in this strange car in this strange place. "What do you mean?"

She sighed, already feeling frustrated with this mission even though it had hardly begun. "You said we're investigating a pride that's distributing illegal weapons. I fully expected some gritty, inner-city scenario with gangs and graffiti and violence in the streets. This looks like something out of a magazine." Leona watched a driver pause and wave a pedestrian through an intersection.

One corner of his mouth lifted. "You should know things aren't always as they seem."

"Oh, you mean like the two of us posing as mates?" She'd resisted saying anything about it during their flight, but she couldn't hold it in anymore. It irritated her on a deep level, like an itch she couldn't reach. "This better not be some ploy on your behalf to get in my pants." Leona folded her arms across her chest.

"Nothing like that," he assured her in that calm, smooth voice of his. "It's just a good cover. Oh, here's the turn." He headed to the left, entering a neighborhood full of sprawling ranch homes on massive lots, each with concrete driveways and two-car garages that faced that road.

"But there are plenty of other options for us," she countered. "Hell, we could even stay in two different houses on different sides of town and cover more territory."

"The cover we've established is the easiest and most likely scenario. From our research, this area is full of humans as well as shifters. To those like us, we're mates. To any humans, we're a married couple.

Either way, we moved to the area for my job. It's simple, and that means it's more likely to be successful."

"It just seemed old-fashioned. And sexist." She wasn't going to change a thing. It was far too late, and Leona knew perfectly well that she'd have to cooperate if she wanted this job with the SOS Force. Just because they'd agreed to send her on this mission and allowed her to have a mental link with them didn't mean they couldn't kick her out anytime they wanted to. This was a probationary period, a test. She needed to pass, and then maybe she could avoid going on any future assignments with just Hudson. She'd been incredibly aware of him as they'd waited in line at the airport, as he'd sat in the seat immediately next to her on the plane with their arms unavoidably touching, and as he'd opened the door of the rental car for her.

"You're thinking about it too much. Ah, here we go." Hudson turned into a driveway and parked in front of the garage. He shut off the ignition and steadied those light brown eyes on her. "Ready to see your new home?"

She gave him a sour look but got out of the car. "Whoa." The place was gorgeous. The brick home had a spacious front yard with carefully maintained landscaping. The covered front porch looked like the perfect place to come out in the early morning for a cup of coffee. This looked more like a vacation home than a temporary place to stay in the field.

Hudson grinned, which only made his features even more striking. "Yeah, not too bad, huh? I can't say anything about how you'll like the inside, though. You never know what you get when you have a local designer fill it with furniture and wall hangings."

Leona started to question him on going to so much trouble for a place they would only be in for a short while, but she clamped her mouth shut. He was a tenured member of the Force, and she'd already been questioning him enough. She followed him inside to find a wide living room with hardwood floors. The place had an open floor plan that lead into the kitchen, allowing people in the two rooms to converse easily. As Hudson had promised, someone had come in and decorated the place with dark leather furniture, a thick rug, and a gleaming dining table. "It's...beautiful."

He closed the door behind them. "I've seen it all online, but we might as well explore the place before we start unloading everything."

Leona nodded, and they headed down the hallway. It held two guest bedrooms on the left, each already equipped with a simple twin bed and basic furniture. "This one will be perfect for setting up the surveillance equipment," she commented. "Big windows, no trees. If we push the bed over to the side, we could even fit an extra worktable in here."

He nodded his approval before they continued on. The guest bathroom was relatively large, and it was right next to the master suite. The hired designer had arranged a massive four-poster bed, the comforter as elaborate as a tapestry. The dresser and mirror were of higher quality than the other bedrooms, made of a beautiful mahogany.

Leona didn't bother peeking into the walk-in closet or the bathroom. She'd seen enough, and she didn't want to make things any more awkward than they already were.

A stairway off the kitchen served as the access to the finished, walkout basement. The backyard was even bigger than the front, and the vinyl fence abutted a wooded area. "This is really nice," she breathed.

Hudson stood next to her on the back porch. The sun was just beginning to set, and the rays gleamed in his hair. "We won't exactly be roughing it, will we?"

His smile was kind. He'd been trying to get along with her, and Leona knew she'd made it a bit difficult. There was no point in arguing with something that couldn't be changed. "No, not really. Let's get our stuff."

Hudson pulled the car into the garage and shut the overhead door before they dared bring in the surveillance equipment—which Leona had been told was all secretly developed by Taylor Communications. Their own bags followed as well. Leona hesitated behind him, letting him claim which room he wanted first. When he'd headed into the master, she turned left into a guest room.

She'd always been low maintenance, so it didn't take long to fill the drawers with her neatly folded clothes and a few simple hygiene items. Leona looked around, knowing she could deal with this. It wasn't what she expected, but that didn't mean it was bad. She had to give this the best chance to succeed, because if she couldn't be a part of the SOS Force, she'd be forced to find something else, something that probably didn't exist. Plus, she'd have to listen to Tracy blather on about backup plans and settling down. *Pfft.*

She was just sliding her suitcase under the bed when she heard Hudson cursing softly to himself.

Leona poked her head out in the hallway. "What's wrong?"

"Nothing really," came a slightly impatient answer. "I just forgot my hair gel."

It was difficult not to laugh at him. "Think you'll survive? Or should we call D.C. for backup?"

He cast a derisive glance over his shoulder. "It's a close call, but I think I can handle it."

Once they'd gotten the monitoring equipment set up, Hudson sat down in the living room and picked up the remote control. But Leona wasn't ready to just relax. She paced the house, studying the way the neighborhood looked from every window, from every angle. She measured the perimeter of both the front and back yards from with her strides, watching the neighbor's houses and taking note of which vehicles went to which houses.

It was a beautiful home in a beautiful neighborhood, and even the man she was there with was beautiful. There was nothing for her to worry about. Even the worst problem the local prides might be dealing with couldn't possibly be as dangerous and dramatic as what she'd seen in her time with the Army. This should be Leona's time to relax, knowing that she had a job to do despite her injury and everything was going to be all right again.

But it didn't feel like it was going to be all right. The lion inside her rolled and shifted. When she was close to Hudson, she knew it was because of him. But her feline traits were still unable to merely settle down in a warm spot and fall asleep. She rubbed her arms and paced, drifting in and out of the rooms of the house, feeling like she was looking for something.

When she stood in front of the kitchen sink, just watching darkness take over the neighborhood, Leona sensed a pair of eyes watching her. She turned, finding Hudson standing next to the breakfast bar. "Hey."

"Hey." He took several steps forward before he hesitated. "Are you okay?"

Again with that question, but it was different coming from his lips. He wasn't asking about her leg, which hadn't even been mentioned since she'd been accepted onto the Force. She cleared her throat. "Yeah, mostly."

"It's hard when you have to adjust to normal life again." Hudson came fully into the kitchen now and opened a cabinet. Apparently, the same people he'd hired to fill the place with furniture had also stocked it with groceries, because he took down a can of coffee and began filling the coffee maker. "I remember coming home like a vivid dream. I knew I should've been happy. I was with my family again. I didn't have to put my life on the line anymore. I wouldn't be seeing all the blood and devastation on a daily basis, but I just wasn't happy."

She stared at him. Was he reading her mind? "Who says I'm not happy?"

Hudson smiled. "C'mon. You and I might have had different specialties, but we've both been through a lot of training. You don't think I've noticed all that pacing? Heard you sigh?"

Leona hadn't even realized she'd been sighing. "I just don't know how to get settled here. It's strange to be on a mission when we're not establishing a rotation for guard duty and rationing out MREs."

"I get it." He took two mugs from a rack on the wall and a bottle of creamer from the fridge and then nodded toward the stools at the breakfast bar. "Sit."

She pursed her lips. He might be considered her senior officer in this scenario, but that didn't mean he could tell her what to do.

Hudson was watching her, waiting. "You've already worn tracks in the hardwood," he commented, tipping one corner of his mouth up. "I just want to talk."

The coffee was brewing, filling the kitchen with that gorgeous scent. "Okay. We can talk. I was thinking we need to find a good way to really get a feel for the neighborhood. You said there are humans and shifters alike here, which means we need to not only figure out who's who but also what they're involved in. There's nothing saying the pride isn't including humans in their scheme, and—"

"Slow down," Hudson said calmly, his voice a soothing rumble from his chest. "We've just got here. No one expects us to do all that right now. There's plenty of time to get started in the morning."

"But we might be missing out on some great opportunities," Leona countered. "What if there's a conversation going on right now that we should be listening to? And don't you think we should be establishing the patterns of the neighborhood? The comings and goings?"

"No, I think we need to be establishing what life is actually going to be like for you now that you're out of the service." He poured them each a mug of the bitter dark liquid and took the stool next to her. "It's not easy, and you need to know that it's all right for it not to be easy."

He was so close, and she could sense every

muscle, every sinew of his body. She couldn't talk to him about this. "I'm fine."

"You're not fine. You're still on guard. You're watching every face you pass, wondering who's going to betray you, who's going to turn out to be the enemy. You're wondering how you can possibly miss a life that had you sleeping on the ground with your gun under your arm, but you miss it anyway. You're wondering how regular people can just carry on with their lives as though there aren't children starving and innocent people being blown to bits on the other side of the world." Hudson swirled creamer into his mug, watching the color of the drink change.

"Yeah." Leona blinked, surprised that a tear had made it through her lashes. Damn him for looking into her soul like that! But he wasn't wrong. "I just don't know if I can do this. I don't mean the mission."

"I know exactly what you mean, and there are thousands of other soldiers who know it, too. Can I give you a little advice?"

She closed her eyes, thinking she could listen to that voice forever. It was low and strong and smooth and so...comforting. "Sure."

"Do you remember what it was like when you first went overseas?"

Leona put the creamer in her own coffee until it was the color of sand. "Exciting. Terrifying. I'd known for a long time that I wanted to join the Army. I'd been getting myself ready for it for a long time, but once I actually got out there—because training didn't count—I wondered what I'd gotten myself into." She'd never admitted that to anyone other than herself. She hadn't wanted to, because it made her sound like a failure compared to everything her father and her uncle had done. It was impossible to imagine that they'd ever been scared of anything.

"So, it was overwhelming, right?" Hudson was still looking down into his coffee.

Leona was grateful not to have those eyes on her right now. His gaze was too intense, and the conversation was intense enough. "Yeah. Pretty much." She let out a small laugh. "The Army changed me a lot, I guess."

"It does that to all of us," Hudson assured her, "and then we have to figure out how to change back when we're done. It's not like we can just melt back into society, as though none of it ever happened. It seems impossible to ever be 'normal' again, but it also seemed impossible at one time to get used to being a soldier and dealing with war. If you could get through that, then you can get through this."

She ran a hand over her forehead and sipped her coffee. "I guess that's true."

"Sure it is. And for me, I had the chance to *think* about life after discharge, because I knew I wasn't reupping. It probably wasn't the same for you."

Leona felt her muscles relaxing, releasing tension she hadn't even realized she was carrying around. It was a relief to talk to someone who actually understood what was going on inside her, even if she hadn't totally understood it herself until she'd said it out loud. "No, it really wasn't. I was going to do it for as long as they would let me, and even once I got too old to stay in the field, I figured I'd train the new recruits. I couldn't see myself at a desk job until I was almost dead."

Hudson nodded. "I can understand that. For me, I knew I was going to be at a desk because of my interest in communications. Sure, there's some time out in the field, but not a ton. I was all right with that. But even if you're not, there's still plenty you can do to keep yourself from feeling useless and bored. The SOS Force was a good start with that, although I'm still a little miffed that you managed to find us so easily."

"I have a few talents," Leona replied, allowing a smug smile to cross her face. "And maybe that's something we can work on when we're done here."

"Whatever you did, it went a long way toward getting you on the team. We really weren't looking for another member, and I don't think any of us had even entertained the idea. But someone with your record and your talent was hard to pass up."

She didn't have time to enjoy the compliment. A knock sounded on the front door, and all the tension instantly returned to her muscles. No one should have known they were there. They weren't expecting any visitors.

"I'll get it," Hudson offered.

But she knew she needed to do this. Hudson had been completely right about adjusting to civilian life. At one point she hadn't been sure she could truly be a soldier, but she'd done it anyway. Now she could force herself to undo it. "No, it's all right. I've got it."

Still, her blood pounded in her veins as she made her way to the front door. She'd kept a small pistol tucked in the back of her waistband once they'd arrived, but it wouldn't be much in the way of defense depending on what was on the other side of that door. She forced her fingers around the knob and opened it.

"Hi!" chirped a perky woman on the doorstep. Her brilliant red hair was coiffed into a knot on the back of her head, and she wore enough make up for two people. The look was topped off with a sequined tank top and tight jeans. "I'm Kim Hartford, and this is my husband Kevin. We just live down the street and thought we'd come say welcome to the neighborhood!" She held out a glass casserole dish with a red cover.

Kevin looked like he'd just gotten home from work, wearing a slightly wrinkled suit and a loose tie. "We've been watching all the moving trucks go in and out, and Kim here just couldn't wait to see who was moving in. Kim grabbed me and practically dragged me down the sidewalk as soon as I got home from work."

Leona was studying them, looking for any signs that they weren't who they said they were. But she didn't detect a bulge of weapons under their clothing or a wire that had slipped loose from its microphone. She plastered a smile on her face. "That's very nice of you. I'm Leona. Hank is in the other room." They'd agreed that they couldn't go by his true name, considering that he owned such a large company. She accepted the casserole dish, but she knew all the food inside it would likely be going in the trash.

"We're getting the whole neighborhood together for a block party at our house on Friday night," Kevin said, pointing over his shoulder down the street. "We'd love for the two of you to come."

It seemed so strange to hear people say such normal, friendly things when she was on a mission. Leona reminded herself once again that she'd just have to learn to deal with it. "Thank you. We'll be there."

"Great! We'll see you then!" Kim trilled. "And if you need anything in the meantime, just holler!"

"Will do. Thanks for stopping by." Leona shut the door and let out a deep breath.

6

"I STILL CAN'T BELIEVE YOU SAID WE'D GO TO THAT block party," Hudson grumbled. He'd had a long night of listening to the neighborhood and figuring out the best places to set up security cameras. They'd been in their "home" for two days, but he still hadn't found anything noteworthy. "I don't have the time to mess around with something like that."

The two of them were in the kitchen, looking through crime reports from St. Louis and the surrounding areas. Leona was bent over the table, frowning at the screen of her tablet, but she looked up at him with a mischievous grin. "We're supposed to be blending in, right? I don't think they would've been very accepting if I'd just told them we were two soldiers who'd only moved into the neighborhood so we could spy on them."

"Of course not. I guess I was just hoping we could keep to ourselves a little bit more." Hudson poured himself another cup of coffee. He'd survived on the stuff in the service, and that habit hadn't changed once he'd come home. In fact, he was pretty sure it'd gotten worse once he'd officially started Taylor Communications. There was always work to be done, and he didn't want to do it halfway.

Leona stood up and stretched, and Hudson immediately averted his eyes. They'd only been in this house together for a short time, but already he found himself thinking about her constantly. If they sat together in the spare bedroom where the surveillance equipment had been set up, he was distracted by his awareness of her body, of her breath, of a gesture as subtle as Leona sweeping a stray lock of hair behind her ear. They ate their meals together at the kitchen table, and he kept his eyes on his plate.

The worst was at night. Leona had taken one of the other small bedrooms for herself without any discussion. Hudson hadn't argued; he liked a big bed and couldn't imagine curling into a tiny ball on one of those twin mattresses. Even with the comfortable four poster bed, he was acutely aware of her presence across the hall. How easy it would be to slip through the doors and to her side, to see her sleep, to bring her back to his own bed where she belonged...

Damn it! He never should've agreed to this mission, not when he knew what was between them. He should've told Drake to pick someone else. Yes, it made sense for him to go since they were in lion territory, but still. The last thing Hudson wanted to do was compromise this mission because he couldn't think with the right head.

"I think the neighbors would be a bit more suspicious if we kept to ourselves." Leona wore her flaxen hair in a loose braid, and she flicked it over her shoulder as she held out her own mug for more coffee. "We don't want to be the mysterious people in the community that everyone's talking about. I do need to talk to you about the block party, though."

"Yeah?" He hoped she would be telling him there was some way of getting out of it. Talking about posing as her mate was one thing, but actually doing it in public would be much harder.

She twisted her mouth, a habit of hers that was surprisingly endearing. "We're supposed to bring a dish."

"Great," he muttered. "Here I was thinking all the

important work would be in figuring out where these weapons were coming from and whether or not the local pride is taking them over the borders of their territory. Turns out my real job is playing Betty fucking Crocker."

Leona put her hands in the air innocently. "Hey, it's not my fault you don't like my cooking."

He shot her a look. "I don't think that's an accurate description of the situation." Leona had tried her hand at cooking dinner the previous night, and it'd been an unmitigated disaster. He'd never had a chance to grimace his way through it, because it was far too burned to be eaten.

"To be fair, I warned you. My mother always did the cooking, and she didn't let the rest of us in the kitchen until she was ready to serve it up. And we both know the Army isn't exactly famous for its culinary culture."

"And that makes *me* the one who gets to cook for all the neighbors? Lucky me." He didn't have time for this. In fact, this whole mission was beginning to look like a waste of time. There hadn't been any indication of suspicious activity in the neighborhood. Everything was so normal it was almost sickening. It hadn't even rained.

The only part of his mission he'd truly been able

to carry out was keeping an eye on Leona. Drake had asked him to do that, but maybe he hadn't meant it in the same way that Hudson was doing it. He couldn't help but keep an eye on her. It was practically torture to have her in the same household. She could be distant and aloof when she was feeling off, but Hudson was quickly learning how to deal with that.

"I'm sure you'll do just fine. I'm going to go get ready." Leona grinned and left the room.

He could hear the shower start a moment later and turned to the fridge, trying to remind himself that this wasn't the first time he'd had to distract himself from his work just to keep his mission going. If he had to throw something together to serve up to the rest of the neighborhood, then so be it. And if he had to go to a party and pretend to just be an average Joe, then he could do that, too. He found all the ingredients he needed for a salad, threw them together in a bowl, and put it in the fridge to chill.

Leona was enclosed in her room when he made his way down the hall to get ready himself. As he passed the open bathroom door, the scented steam crept out into the corridor, making him close his eyes to avoid picturing her naked in the shower. That only made it worse, though. He closed himself into the master suite and ran the coldest shower he could stand.

Hudson wondered what the guys would say if they had any idea what he was going through. It was easy enough for them to all agree that they couldn't get involved with her. They weren't *fated* to her. They didn't feel the unbelievable urge to shift in her presence and claim her. They didn't spend all their extra brain power focusing on a woman who'd been attached to them by something stronger and stranger than any of them could understand.

Well, Drake would understand. He'd found his mate in an unexpected place. But it was too late to ask him about it now, when he'd already agreed to go on this mission with Leona. If he had a problem with it, Hudson should've said something about it before he left D.C.

He huffed out a breath and washed his hair and body, drying off quickly and wrapping himself in a towel before trying to decide what to wear. He'd brought plenty of casual wear, a few more specialized outfits depending on what they might end up doing for the mission, and some comfortable sweats for around the house. All the suits he typically wore to the office were left at home where they belonged. He wasn't Hudson Taylor here. He was Hank Talcott, a simple salesman who'd moved there from the East Coast.

In the end, he settled on a white lightweight button-down with short sleeves paired with khaki cargo shorts. Casual, comfortable, but not too sloppy. Hopefully it would be good enough for Kevin and Kim and the rest of the neighborhood. He combed his hair back, hoping it would stay in place since he hadn't bothered to get out and pick up that hair gel yet. After slipping into a pair of leather sandals, he headed back toward the kitchen.

But a woman was standing in the living room. She wore a blue dress with white polka dots that just skimmed the tops of her knees. Her back was to him, but he could see the way the dress tucked in at her slim waist. Even her shoulder blades were shapely between the wide straps of the dress, and her neck was long and smooth underneath the tendrils of curls that cascaded from her updo. Hudson cleared his throat and she turned.

It was Leona. He'd known it, somewhere deep down, and yet he couldn't quite believe it. He'd never seen her wear anything like that, nor had he expected it. Her typical style didn't seem much different than his own, and she preferred things that were comfortable and utilitarian instead of fashionable. But now, she was dressed like the goddess of summer. Even her face looked different, and he realized she was wearing makeup.

"You...um...you look great," he managed to murmur. "I like your hair."

She bit her lip, accentuating her bright red lipstick as she looked down at her dress. "You don't think it's too much? I brought it along just in case, but I don't want to stand out too much."

He swallowed. It was hard enough being in the house with her, but now that she was in that dress, he didn't know how much longer he could control himself. He turned away toward the kitchen and pulled his dish out of the fridge to give himself something else to do. "No, I'm sure it's perfectly fine."

"I don't think I've ever been to a block party before, unless maybe it was something that my mom dragged me to when I was a kid. I'm not sure what to do with myself." She ran her hands over the skirt of the dress again with uncertainty.

Hudson shrugged, trying to turn this outing back into part of the mission instead of anything that seemed like a date. "Mostly, we'll just have to hang out and be ourselves. Talk to as many people as possible, see what you can find out about them without getting too invasive, eat a bit, have a beer, and then we'll come back home." Even saying "home" sounded too familiar, given that they were nothing but teammates. Teammates. Right.

"You're right. I'm sorry. I don't even know why I'm asking you this. I mean, it's not like I haven't done an undercover mission before. This is just totally different. I'm more comfortable in camo." She touched her hair, obviously having no idea just what she was doing to him.

He uncovered the bowl and picked up a bag of tortilla chips. "Here, try some. Tell me if it needs more salt or anything."

Leona picked up a chip and frowned into the bowl. "What is it?"

"Cowboy caviar. Sounds weird, I know, but it's really good. Beans, corn, tomatoes, avocados, stuff like that." Hudson didn't consider himself a five-star chef, but he knew how to make things that were simple and tasty. Being a bachelor had made him more than sick of drive-thru faire.

He watched as she loaded up her chip and placed it between those luscious lips. Her lined eyes widened in surprise. "Oh! That's really good!" She reached for more.

Hudson turned away. "You'll have to wait until

the party. I'm sure Kevin and Kim will want to try it, too," he said with a grin. "Let's go and get this over with."

The Hartfords' home was similar to their own, brick with a nice front yard and plenty of space. They weren't exactly living in a poor neighborhood, and Hudson wondered if he could ever settle down in a place like this instead of his luxury apartment. It seemed more homelike, more normal, more friendly.

"Hey! You made it!" Kim Hartford clapped her hands together when she opened the door, pulling it open wider to admit them. "Come on in! Just about everyone else is here. We've got the grill going out back. There are plenty of drinks in the fridge, and we're just putting all the food here on the table. Let me introduce you to a few people."

Hudson had told Leona that they were to use the party as part of their mission, but he found it much more difficult than he would've thought. Kim and Kevin seemed genuinely excited about introducing them to the other neighbors. The men gathered around the grill on the back patio while the women laughed in the kitchen. He glanced at Leona a few times to make sure she was holding her own, unable to believe he was there with such a beauty, and then easily got lost in conversations about baseball and road construction.

At one point, he headed out to the back porch after grabbing a beer from the fridge when a woman stepped in front of him. "Oh, excuse me," he said as he tried to step around her.

But she didn't let him. She moved directly back into his path, tipping back her chin and jutting one hip forward. "You just moved in down the street, didn't you?"

"Yeah, sorry. Hank Talbott." He held out his hand.

"Cathy Cooper." She took his hand in both of her own. Her fingers circled his, making their way slowly up his arm. "Mr. Talbott, someone said you were in sales, but I have to wonder what kind of sales would keep you in such good shape." She arched one slim eyebrow that matched her flowing dark hair.

Hudson felt his skin heat. It was flattering, but a little *too* flattering. He didn't know this woman, and he couldn't see any reason for her to be talking to him like this. "I'm in computers."

Cathy practically batted her eyelashes at him. "Oh, that's exciting! Always on the verge of new technology. I'd love to hear more about it. Why don't you come over here with me? There's a lovely little shaded area on the edge of the garden." She began leading him away from the crowd and toward the back corner of the yard.

There was something about this woman he didn't like, and Hudson wasn't about to go disappear with her. "I can't actually, but thanks."

"Ahem."

He turned at the noise behind him to find Leona standing just outside the sliding glass doors. Her cheeks were pink as she glared at Cathy, and her look wasn't any more friendly when she riveted it on Hudson. "I think it's time for us to go, dear."

"So soon?" Cathy pouted.

He managed to untangle himself from her grasp. "Yes, we've got some other things to attend to." Hudson, glad for the excuse, followed Leona back into the house.

"Kim, I'm afraid we've got to get going," Leona said to their hostess. "Thank you for inviting us." She didn't wait for a reply before she headed for the front door.

Hudson had to jog to catch up with her on the sidewalk. They'd chosen to walk to the party, since it was just down the street. It was a gorgeous evening, with a nice breeze blowing away the humidity, but there were also waves of anger billowing off his partner. "Hey, slow down! What's the hurry?"

She surprised him by stopping in her tracks and whirling on him. "What's the hurry? Really? Are you actually going to tell me you don't have a clue what was happening back there?" Leona was a full head shorter than he was, but she'd managed to shove her face within an inch of his as she spoke. Just as quickly as she'd stopped walking, she whirled around and stomped off down the sidewalk again.

Hudson watched her go, allowing himself a chance at a smile. She was clearly pissed, but he only found it flattering. "I don't see what the big deal is," he said innocently when he caught up again. "She was just introducing herself and trying to get to know me, and that was the whole point of this adventure anyway, wasn't it?"

"That *woman* was trying to do a lot more than get to know you." Her brows were knitted together, but she refused to look at him now as she charged toward their house.

"Maybe so, but in that case, I should've gone with her. I mean, what better way to infiltrate the neighborhood and get a feel for what's really going on, right?"

He was grinning when she glared up at him

again. They were right in front of their place now, and she snorted as she let her shoulders drop slightly in defeat. "It may be funny to you, but for all anyone here knows, we're together. Mates, married, common law, whatever the hell you might want to call it. It's rude for someone to assume they can just waltz up and talk to you like that. Takes a lot of balls." She stormed into the house.

Hudson watched her go, admiring the way the dress swished around her thighs. Leona was crazy if she thought he'd be interested in anyone but her, yet he'd enjoyed yanking her chain a little. Sure, maybe it was just the principle of the thing, but he liked the way jealousy looked on her face.

7

Leona couldn't stand another minute inside those perfectly painted walls. The house was beautiful. It was the kind of place that most people probably dreamed of living in, and she had no doubt they'd be willing to take on mortgage payments bigger than what they could actually afford just for the status symbol of a nice home in a nice neighborhood. It even had stainless steel appliances, hardwood floors, and a stone fireplace.

But she absolutely had to get out of there. Her muscles were getting sore from sitting around listening in on phone conversations and keeping track of the various vehicles and people in the neighborhood. She hadn't seen anyone but Hudson since the block party. The walls were beginning to close in on her, and it was time to get out.

She rose early, pulled on leggings and a tank top, and dug her favorite shoes out from under the bed. Leona whipped her hair up into a quick ponytail without even bothering to brush it. Coffee could wait until she got back and had time to enjoy it on the porch, but right now, she had something she absolutely had to do.

It was the perfect morning for a jog. The sun was already beginning to rise in the summer sky, but the commuters hadn't yet left their garages. An old man on the corner was watering his flowers. A dog barked from within a fenced yard. It didn't look like the sort of place she should be doing recon. That, however, is exactly what she told herself she was doing. She was just another part of the scenery, and she'd seen plenty of other people jogging and walking.

When she reached the corner, she took a right and kept going. The park wasn't far, according to the maps she'd studied. Leona stretched her legs out into longer strides, pumping her arms and expanding her lungs. Her jog had turned into a run, and she was sprinting with all her speed before she knew it. God, it felt good! The wind whistled against her ears and combed through her ponytail, gracing her skin and cooling her sweat. She felt free and real, part of the Earth but not part of it at the same time. She veered into the park and circled it, her feet barely touching the asphalt track as she blasted past an elderly woman who was keeping a much more leisurely pace.

"Good morning!" Leona called cheerily behind her. She wanted to laugh, because she couldn't remember a time when she felt this good. Yes, she was on a mission. The enemy could be sitting in the house on her right with the blue shutters and proliferating rose bushes. It could just as easily be the paper boy who'd appeared, chucking rolled up newspapers at front doors with a satisfying thunk. When she stopped in at the little convenience store a few blocks further down for a bottle of Gatorade, she knew the bored man behind the counter or the shifty guy near the beer cooler could also be the enemies she was looking for. She almost didn't care. Leona was happy with any result at the moment. She could kick herself for not getting out and doing this earlier.

Someone was waving at her when she came back around the corner, and Leona noticed it was Kim. She waved back, but Kim was walking toward the fence, waving her down. Leona slowed, catching her breath. "Hey! Beautiful morning!"

"Sure is! I just wanted to check in with you and see if you were doing all right, hun." Kim was dressed in cropped leggings and a loose-fitting tank top with a sports bra underneath. Her hair was pulled back like Leona's was, but it was obvious she'd taken a lot more care with it. She'd curled and teased the red strands to a massive pouf. The layers of makeup on her face indicated she wasn't planning to work out any time soon.

"Sure. I'm fine. Why?" Leona took advantage of the break to stretch. She bent one way and then the other, feeling her muscles gliding under her skin. She'd have to find some time for her other form soon.

Kim made a face, looking concerned. "Well, you and Hank left pretty quickly the other night. Jamie Sandusky said she thought she saw Cathy Cooper talking to your husband, and I was worried. You see, Cathy is quite the flirt. She doesn't mean to hurt anyone, though."

"Oh." Leona was grateful her face was already flushed from her run. She'd been absolutely infuriated when that woman had flirted with Hudson, but that didn't mean she wanted anyone else to know that. "It's fine, really. I'm not the jealous type." How could she be, when she and Hudson weren't anything but coworkers? Right?

Her neighbor didn't look ready to accept that. She leaned on the split rail fence between them, her fingers gliding across a nearby lilac bush. "It's perfectly fine if you are. I mean, it wouldn't be the first time we'd seen some domestic issues in the neighborhood. Nothing major, mind you, but enough to get people talking. It's not a huge town, and we do get to know and care about each other."

"It's very nice around here. And we really enjoyed ourselves at the block party." That was true, up to a point. The women Kim had introduced her to had been very kind to Leona. She'd expected them to treat her like an outsider who didn't know all their secrets and inside jokes, but it wasn't like that at all. The only thing she *had* felt excluded from was the "mom talk" from those who had little ones. And then, of course, there had been that Cathy Cooper incident.

"I'm glad. I really was worried, but I didn't want to rush over there and get in your way. I'm sure your busy with all the unpacking."

"No, not really." Leona wrapped her arm around her head to stretch all the little muscles that hadn't had a good workout in ages. "It was all taken care of before we moved in."

"It was?" Kim said with disbelief. "I guess I underestimated the two of you when you said your husband is in computer sales. A service like that costs a lot of money."

Shit. She was getting too comfortable, and she'd slipped already. "What I mean," Leona said, "is that we had the movers take care of the furniture, but we didn't have much else to bring in. We're sort of minimalists."

"Oh, yes! I've heard of that. I don't think I could ever do without my shoe collection," Kim laughed.

Leona laughed along with her, glad she'd gotten out of that one.

Kim smiled happily as she plucked one of the lilacs and held it to her nose. "Now tell me about your plans for the future, Leona. Are the two of you going to have any children?"

"No way," she answered automatically. "It would really interfere with my job."

The neighbor's auburn brows knitted together. She laughed uncomfortably. "I'm sorry. I could swear you told me at the party that you stay at home."

"I did. I mean, I do." Shit. How could she be screwing this up so badly. Leona had successfully performed numerous undercover missions that required her to successfully infiltrate enemy territory. This one should be much easier, and yet it was somehow proving to be the complete opposite. "I do stay at home right now, but I plan to get a job soon. I like to get out and interact with the world."

"Oh, I see. I understand. It's not always easy taking care of my own and never having any time for myself, but I manage here and there. You really should think about children, though. They're so wonderful. I don't know how I ever managed without them." Just then, two kids came tumbling through the front door and onto the porch. Leona recognized them as Kim's offspring, who were introduced at the block party, but she couldn't remember their names.

The oldest had his younger brother in a headlock. "Mom! He took my tablet and he won't give it back!"

"I only took it because he took mine first!" the younger one squealed. He might've looked like he had the disadvantage with his older brother's arm around his neck, but one quick stomp to the instep and he was free. Leona had to smile at that.

A little girl poked her head out the door and, seeing that her older siblings were otherwise occupied, stepped down off the porch and began picking flowers from the bushes in the landscaping. She was still in her bright pink pajamas.

"Boys! Stop that right now!" Kim's fists curled at the arrival of her kids, and she turned an embarrassed smile to Leona. "Like I said, such angels. I'd better get them off to school before they kill each other. See you later!"

Leona jogged on home catching the angry undertones from her neighbor as she got onto her children. Kim had brought up an interesting point. Leona hadn't worried much about having children. Her career had always been first, and she'd always known it would be. But what, exactly, was her career now? Would working with the SOS Force preclude her from becoming a mother? Was that something she even wanted? It was an idea she'd never allowed herself to ponder before.

Hudson met her at the door, the muscles of his jaw twitching as he pressed his teeth together. "There you are!"

"Yes, here I am!" she exploded. Even the strange conversation with Kim hadn't ruined the good mood from her jog. "You should get out and see this neighborhood. It's like something from a movie. That really bothered me at first, but I'm starting to like it. Is there any coffee?" She headed into the kitchen.

"There is." His presence was like a heavy shadow behind her, and when Leona finished pouring, she turned to see him still glowering. "Why didn't you tell me you were leaving the house?"

"Excuse me?" Leona slowly stirred her creamer into her coffee, smiling at the sheer audacity of this man.

"You heard me. You can't just disappear, Leona. I had no idea where you were or what happened to you. You didn't even take your phone!" He put his hands on his hips as he paced the kitchen. "You clearly don't know just how important this mission is."

"I do," she countered. Her muscles tensed despite her efforts to keep calm, and she felt the good effects of her jog swiftly being undone. "In fact, that's exactly why I left. I needed to get out of here before I went crazy. It wouldn't look normal if I never left the house. And it was a good chance for recon."

"And for nearly giving away our secret to the nosiest neighbor," Hudson retorted.

"Wait, what?" She stared at him for a moment before it dawned on her. "You were using the surveillance equipment to spy on me?" Leona was used to having a life that was less than private. Her position as a Green Beret meant she'd spent plenty of time being poked, prodded, and watched. That was all right, because she'd agreed to it. This was different.

Hudson threw one hand in the air, fingers spread. "What choice did you leave me? I woke up and you were just gone! I had no idea when you were coming back, or even if you'd left of your own free will! I heard you talking to Kim, and that was the only thing that kept me from calling in the rest of the Force to track you down."

"Wow." Leona set her mug on the counter and rubbed her knuckles against her thigh, feeling the itch of her claws threatening to make their appearance. They were desperate to break through and scratch him right across his face for his comments and his arrogance. "You've got some nerve. You might be my commanding officer, for all intents and purposes, but you don't run my life. If I want to go for a jog, then that's exactly what I'm going to do. And if I want to talk to the neighbor, then I'm going to do that as well. And I've also decided that I need to have a job while I'm here."

"What?" He blinked, thrown off by the last demand.

"You just decided when we planned out this mission that I would be a housewife. That's not going to work for me. None of these people know who I really am, but that means I can be whomever I want to be. Maybe I've got my degree in education and I want to be a teacher. Maybe I'm a really good artist and I sell my paintings online." The possibilities seemed endless to her now that she was thinking about it, and she liked them more and more as she spoke. There wasn't anything to stop her.

Except him, apparently. Hudson let out an impatient sigh as he stepped around the breakfast bar toward her. "We didn't plan for that because it wasn't important. It's still not."

"It is to me." She narrowed her eyes as she looked up at him, fully aware at just how far she'd thrust her chin forward.

Another step, and she could feel the heat off his body as he loomed over her. "It's not important to the mission, and it's not happening. You know as well as I do that we can't go changing things in the middle of the mission."

"I'll do what I want," she asserted. The tension was building between them, a thick force in the air that was nearly palpable. Leona felt her lioness thrashing and clawing inside her, insisting that she continue this fight against such a stubborn male.

"You won't," he snarled. "You'll do as I tell you. Nothing more and nothing less."

"Don't you dare tell me what to do." They were face to face now, their skin only an inch apart.

"I just did." Hudson emitted a low growl.

It reverberated through her body. She felt every breath she took, the air being pulled out of her lungs as every cell of her body came to life. Her hands and feet sparked with a pulsing energy that made her body difficult to control. It was too much. Her tongue pressed against her teeth as she tried to decide if she would burst with the overload of being so close to her destiny or if she would lash out against him for making her feel this way.

Deep down, Leona knew the true answer. Her body and the universe were telling her one thing, but her job demanded something different. It didn't matter how attracted she was to Hudson, or if he was attracted to her. He was difficult and possessive and just plain impossible, but he was very right about one thing. They were on a mission. That came first. She could tamp down everything else and worry about it later.

She sidestepped to the left, snatched the small

bag from the corner store and tossed it at him as she walked away. "I bought you some hair gel. I'm taking a shower." Leona stormed out of the room and down the hall, not knowing how the hell she was going to get through this.

8

Hudson had been buried in the "guest" bedroom for a long time. He couldn't be sure just how much time had passed, considering how little had been happening. The neighborhood had been eerily quiet, and he didn't like it. He'd spent all day listening to husbands and wives bidding each other goodbye before they went to work. Some of them were loving and sweet, and some of them fought (with promises to continue the fight that evening). He heard kids talking about their crushes at school. During that time, at least, there had been something to listen to. The middle of the day in the neighborhood had only produced a few daytime soap operas. He monitored internet traffic and cell phone conversations without finding much that was more exciting. As the day moved toward the afternoon, he heard those same children coming home from school and those same husbands and wives reuniting as they returned home from work. Some of them did continue their arguments, and others made up.

It was at that point that Hudson realized he'd spent far too long sitting in one spot. His body ached, and he was irritated.

The lack of intelligence was irritating, but even more than that, he was still pissed at Leona. It'd been a full day since their argument. There was no reason to stay mad about it. It was over. But he couldn't seem to let it go.

If it was anyone else, he wouldn't be thinking about it anymore. He wasn't the kind to hold a grudge. He dealt with his problems and then he moved on. But there was something so completely different between him and Leona. He'd absolutely panicked when he'd gotten up the previous morning and found her missing. He'd gone through the entire house looking for her, sure that she couldn't have just left. She knew what this mission was all about. She knew how important it was. She knew what was on the line, including her permanent position with the Force. And if she hadn't just left on her own, that meant something else had happened to her.

That was the worst thought of all. He'd brought her there, knowing there was a possibility of danger, knowing just what they were to each other. She had to know it, too, but that was beside the point. Without discussing it, Hudson knew it was his job to keep her safe. Even if you took the whole fated part out of the equation, he was the one who had experience with the Force.

As he'd checked the basement, the backyard, and the bedrooms, his blood had raced through his body with such force, it made him dizzy. He felt the shiver of fur that burst through his skin on the back of his neck, a sign of his other form as it demanded to come through and take care of this.

Fortunately, he'd finally found reason and logic again when he'd sat down to listen to the neighborhood and located her just down the street. No matter how many times he'd told himself that it was all right, that knowledge hadn't taken away the anger that had come along with his dismay at finding her gone.

He'd hardly seen her at all after that, even though they were supposed to be working together. He imagined that she was off hiding and pouting instead of just acting like a mature adult, but he knew he was doing the same thing.

As if his thoughts had summoned her, the door to the bedroom opened. Leona leaned against the doorway, her face a mask. "I ordered some pizza. Should be here in about half an hour, and I thought I should give you a heads up."

He took off one side of his headphones and considered asking her if that was a dig at him, but he let it go. "Sounds good. I'll be out in a minute. Hold on." Hudson slapped the headphones back on, listening intently.

"We're meeting down by the river. He says he's got a small boat."

Hudson worked quickly at his monitor, pinpointing the voice as coming from Kevin and Kim's house. But he'd already known that. He recognized Kevin's voice right away. It figured that the cleanest, nicest people in the area would be the culprits. He gestured for Leona to pick up the other set of headphones.

"You sure about this?" the other voice asked. It was another man, one Hudson didn't recognize as readily. "I mean, it's one thing to just hand over a few guns out of the back of a van, but—"

"Hey, I said I would get all our money back, didn't I?" Kevin demanded.

Hudson knew from experience that the man probably wasn't angry as much as anxious. People got themselves into these situations and didn't know how to get back out, and that was how one small opportunity turned into a lifetime of crime.

"Yeah," the second voice sighed. "I don't like it, though. It sounds dangerous."

"It's no more dangerous than everything else we've been doing. Just make sure you keep your fucking mouth shut. We might be making good money for the pride, but I don't want some loudmouth to expose us. Here's what we're going to do…"

Hudson and Leona were perfectly still as they listened. The equipment was automatically recording it all for them, and they could review it as many times as they needed to. When the second man left Kevin's house and the conversation turned to what Kim was going to fix for dinner and when the boys had their next baseball game, Hudson finally took off his headphones. "I guess we've got our first lead."

Leona smiled, a beautiful look on her that he didn't see often enough. "I think this is what we needed. And I can't say I'm surprised. Kevin seems like the type, and so does Sean."

"Ah, you've got a good ear. I knew I'd heard the voice, but I hadn't recognized it." He'd met Sean at the block party, a highway engineer who was quiet and reserved. Definitely the nerdy type. These guys were in over their heads.

"He doesn't talk much, but he has a very distinct accent when he does. Like he's lived here for a long time, but he's originally from a different area." Her eyes shone with intrigue as she spoke, a reflection of how excited she got simply by doing her job.

"Well, you're definitely right that this is what we needed. It's difficult sitting behind enemy lines without doing anything. Now, let's see. They're meeting up at midnight. That gives me plenty of time to prepare. I'll take a minimal amount of equipment, basically just enough to record everything that happens. I don't plan to intercept anything at this time, and—"

"Hold on a second." The smile had been wiped clean from her face. "I don't like the way this sounds."

"What do you mean?" He didn't want to deal with female drama again. He had important work to do, and he could tell by the look on her face that she was more concerned about arguing with him again.

"You're talking like you're going to do this on your own," she replied, her eyes narrowing.

Damn her, she was sexy even when she was angry with him. He cleared his throat. "Yes. I am. There's no point in the two of us going when it's a one-man job."

"Somehow, I have a feeling that's not quite the case." She'd sat down to listen to the conversation, but she stood up again now, folding her arms in front of her chest. "I'm going with you."

His mind flashed through all the possibilities, fueled by his terror when he'd found her missing the previous day. There were so many things that could happen. What if they were caught? What if they were found out and the enemy captured her? Flint and Garrison were still in D.C., and Drake had probably returned to California by now. It would take far too long to get any backup there, and he couldn't risk it. "It's a smarter idea for you to stay here. You're less experienced, and—"

"Don't feed me that bullshit," she snapped. "I've got plenty of experience under my belt, or else you and the others never would've let me on the Force. You don't just recruit people off the street, or really even at all. You've seen my service record, and it doesn't even list the details of the work I did."

Hudson pulled in a deep breath, trying to keep his patience. "That may be true, but you and I both know this is a completely different situation than when you were actively in the service. I shouldn't have to remind you that you nearly gave yourself away yesterday."

"I think that's a bit of an exaggeration. I messed up, but I never said anything about who we really are or what we're here for. *We.*" She emphasized the last word just as a spark of anger flashed in her eyes.

He couldn't really blame her for being angry, but that didn't make him feel any better about the situation. He wanted to kick himself for thinking she was any less capable of this. It made him look like such a sexist ass, even though her gender had absolutely nothing to do with his decision. Hudson bit the inside of his cheek, fighting the urge to stand up, pin her against the wall, and tell her exactly who was in charge. That wasn't going to improve their working conditions, though. "Yeah. You're right."

She nodded, looking a little surprised at changing his mind so quickly. "Good. Let's eat some pizza, and then we can come up with a plan."

Hudson followed her out of the room, having

been so engrossed in his thoughts that he'd nearly missed the sound of the delivery car pulling up the driveway.

Hudson crouched on the hill that lead down to the river, where a small boat bobbed in the water at anchor. One light on the bow indicated its presence and that someone occupied it, otherwise it might've gone completely unseen in the night.

Kevin and Sean had done their best to go unnoticed as they made their way to the meeting spot. They'd left their homes at different times and had taken different routes down to the waterfront. Anyone else might not have noticed them or thought anything about their little trip, but Hudson and Leona knew exactly what they were up to. They'd ensconced themselves not far from the riverbank just inside the tree line.

"Looks like Sean is backing up his van," Leona whispered, a pair of binoculars pressed to her face. "They've got crates back there. Let's see if they open them up." She sounded just as excited to be out in the field for this mission as he was.

Hudson had to admit it was a nice break from

being cooped up in the house. Plus, this felt like they were actually making progress. He hadn't yet had proof that the trafficking was interfering with another pride as had been claimed, but they knew for sure now that their time in Illinois wasn't being wasted. "I've got the mics and cameras ready for recording. With just a little bit of luck, we're going to have a great lead on this in just a few minutes."

He felt Leona's body tense beside him. "You know, there are just the three of them." She continued to watch through the lenses, her front teeth grabbing her lower lip.

"And?"

"And?" She dropped the binoculars and gave him a mischievous glance. "And it wouldn't take any effort for us to just take them down."

"That's not what we're here to do, Leona."

She sighed and shifted slightly in the grass. "C'mon, don't tell me you haven't thought about it. Let's say we went down there in human form. You've got two soldiers against a couple of suburban dads and whoever their buyer is."

"That's just the thing. We haven't even seen the buyer yet. We don't even know for sure how many people are on that boat." Granted, unless they were packed in there like sardines, there couldn't be very many.

"Fair enough, but what if we went down there in a different guise? There's no question of just how much damage we could do." Her voice was deep and sexy as she spoke, and she nudged her body a little closer to Hudson's. "You must've been thinking about it. I know I have."

There was nothing more he would've liked than to shift into his other form, to let his muscles lengthen and strengthen, to feel the wind through his mane. Actually, there was one thing he would like more, and that would be to do that with Leona. Hudson could easily imagine himself barreling down the hill alongside her, their claws digging into the ground for traction as they built up speed, their spines stretching as they made the jump from the small dock to the boat, their teeth sinking into flesh as they tore apart the enemy.

And he would love to see how she looked in that form again. Their entire relationship up until this point had been careful and programmed, the two of them walking in slow circles as they sized each other up. He knew that a glorious lioness was within her—he had seen evidence of it in the flash of her eyes and the flick of animal instinct in her shoulder.

He could easily remember what she'd looked like in the firelight on that night they'd accepted her into the Force, but that didn't mean he'd mind a refresher.

Hudson shook his head, pissed that he'd allowed himself to get distracted. "We can't do that. We've got to gather all the information we can before we act, and you know that."

"I do, but I'm bored," she admitted with a smile.

Okay, good. At least they were back on good terms with each other. That was something. "Listen," he whispered as someone came out of the boat's cabin.

He was a heavy man, and a swarthy one, even in the darkness. He spoke with an accent that Hudson recognized. The humid air had created a thin slick of sweat over the surface of his skin, but it felt frozen as soon as he'd heard that voice. Either Leona recognized the accent as well, or she'd just finally decided to take this task seriously, because she was quiet and still as a stone.

"My friends!" the buyer said, spreading his arms wide. "You're just on time. Let's see what you've brought me." He stepped off the boat and up to the back of Sean's van, nodding as the man opened one of the small crates. "Wonderful. Just wonderful."

"We thought you'd be pleased," Kevin said with a boyish grin. "Now there's a matter of the payment."

"Of course." The buyer returned to his boat and came back with a small briefcase. "Let's get these unloaded."

"Hang on." Kevin stepped between the man and the goods. "I'd like some time to count this first."

"You don't trust me, my friend?" The jovial tone of the buyer's voice had reduced somewhat.

Hudson swallowed, understanding that this deal was about to go south. "You might get your wish after all. We'll have to get them out of there if they do something stupid."

She nodded but didn't answer, her eyes still glued on the exchange.

"Come on, Husam. We can all be reasonable here." Kevin opened the briefcase.

Hudson tensed, waiting for things to go haywire. It made sense that Kevin would want to count the money, just as this Husam guy would probably want to check the inventory that was being given to him. But it was clear neither side trusted each other, and he wouldn't have been surprised if the buyer took that pistol tucked in the back of his pants and blew the suburbanite away.

Instead, he shrugged impatiently as Kevin

counted the money and began pulling the small crates from the back of the van. "I don't have time to wait for you to count your pennies."

It wasn't as though Hudson hadn't seen plenty of people killing each other, but he was still relieved to know this was just the typical tension involved with an illegal exchange. As far as Hudson knew, the transaction had nothing to do with other clans in the area, but he could run all the information through the computer once they got back home and go from there. He had pictures, video, and audio recordings of all parties involved. That was what he needed.

Leona's hand clamped down on his wrist. He looked up to see that she'd put the binoculars down, her eyes glistening in the starlight as she looked over Hudson's shoulder, further down the bank.

He dared to swing his head, and he now saw what she saw. The buyer was the only one on the boat. They'd been right about that guess. But he wasn't the only one in the area. Other men had moved in, creeping stealthily through the woods along the river to watch the interchange just as he and Leona had. They'd come armed to the teeth, their automatic rifles held at the ready, and there were plenty of them.

Fuck! Hudson glanced back down at the river,

where Kevin had finished fiddling with the cash and was now helping Sean load all the boxes on the boat's deck. Things were going smoothly down there, for now. What did the buyer have planned? Were these forces simply an extra precaution against a seller they were unused to dealing with? Or were they there to recover the money once the weapons were safely loaded, ensuring they and their boss didn't lose out on this deal?

He signaled to Leona, and the two of them began working quickly to put their equipment away. They had what they needed, and so far, they hadn't been seen. Hudson had counted at least a dozen of them, far more than the two of them could take on alone. He had little confidence that Kevin and Sean could or would help them. They'd have to get out of there.

The dark figures were gliding their way. There was no telling yet if this was simply their plan or if they'd spotted the infiltrators, but either way, it wasn't good.

Leona cinched her bag shut and touched his arm once again. She leaned back into the shadows, her form changing from a compact human one to a sleek feline one. Her black clothing melted away into that pale golden fur, which took on the bluish hue of the starlight. Her eyes had changed to those of her lioness, but they kept their gaze on him as she grabbed her bag in her teeth.

They didn't need to speak to understand each other, and she was right. They stood no chance against these men. He didn't like to leave anyone to their own devices if he could help it, but their job right now was to make sure the intelligence they'd gathered made it back to the Force for processing. They had a much greater chance of doing so if they left on four feet instead of two.

Hudson did the same. It was easy to shift even with so many enemies surrounding them, because he'd always felt more comfortable and powerful when he knew he could rely on his own natural weapons. He followed Leona back through the trees.

Think we should drop off the equipment and get back there? she asked.

It was the first time they'd communicated that way since the ceremony, and it startled Hudson to hear her voice in his head like that. He wasn't used to it. He hesitated for a moment before answering. If he'd been out here with his men, he wouldn't have hesitated. They were used to fighting side by side. They knew the risks and they were willing to accept them. Technically, that was true for Leona as well, but once again, everything was different with her.

He'd come to realize just how much he needed her and worried for her. He wanted to protect her with everything he had, to literally put his body in the way of anything that might harm her.

No. I don't think they're in any more danger than they would've been if we hadn't shown up. Those guys are just backup in case things go badly. Let's get out of here and go home.

9

"I don't like this. It's not a good idea."

Leona tipped her chin up to look at Hudson. He was supposed to be her partner out there on this mission, but he was proving to be more of a hindrance than anything. It'd been less than a day since they'd returned from their spy mission down by the river, a task which she'd thought had gone fairly well, and yet he was back to being stubborn and overly cautious. "I *do* think it's a good idea. I know how you feel, Hudson, but we can't let feelings get in the way of what we're trying to do."

His eyes grazed over her hair, which she'd pulled back in a similar style to what she'd done for the block party. She'd told herself as she'd looked in the mirror that she'd only done it because it would help her blend in, and not because he'd liked it.

"But we've got *proof* that these people are involved in trafficking. What we saw at the river is probably just a small sample of what they've been doing. We can't just waltz into their house like it's not a big deal, like we didn't see what we saw last night."

"It's exactly because of what we saw last night that I'm taking Kim up on her invitation." Her neighbor had called up that morning after breakfast, inviting Leona over for lunch.

"You have to admit that the timing is a little strange." Hudson crossed his arms in front of his chest, making himself look even bigger and more intimidating than he did anyway.

"Maybe." Leona had thought of that. It did seem odd that she should get invited over right after she and Hudson had been spying on her husband, but there was no evidence that anyone had seen them. And Kevin's sedan had gone gliding down the street at precisely o-seven-hundred hours that morning. "If it is, then I'll only make us look more suspicious by refusing to go. And it's just lunch."

"I guess that's true. And I'll be listening from this end."

She looked up at him. Hudson was a brawny man, and when he was living his normal life, he was in charge of a massive company. She'd understood he had a reputation as a man who possessed a lot of drive but executed it calmly. The side of him Leona was seeing seemed a bit different. It was nice of him to worry over her, if she could get past those old-fashioned gender rules, but she didn't need it. "I wish you wouldn't."

"Leona..."

"Fine, fine!" She threw her hands in the air, giving up. He was right, even if she didn't like it. "I guess that's better than wearing a wire."

Hudson tipped his head to one side as his eyes traced down her body. "That would be more accurate, though, and it would fit nicely under that blouse..."

"Stop it!" She turned away from him, ostensibly to pick up her purse. "It'll be fine. But keep in mind that if you listen in on our lunch, then we're wasting our manpower. I'll already be there, so I'll know what's happening. You could be listening to other households."

His lips tightened into a hard line, and Leona could tell she had him there. He didn't want to admit she was right, but that was fine. She knew it.

"I'll be back in an hour or so, and I promise I'll give you the full report of all the super weird and damning things she does while I'm there." Leona left in a huff, wondering if she would ever get used to working with the man.

And about half an hour later, Leona had nearly forgotten that he was waiting for her just down the street, listening to every word she said. She'd thought it would be awkward for a soldier to have a good conversation with a wife and mother who'd never seen anything more dangerous than the evening news. But over Kim's homemade martinis, the two were enjoying finger sandwiches and conversation that touched on a little bit of everything.

"She's an absolute doll," Leona commented of Kim's little girl as her neighbor returned from down the hall, where she'd laid her youngest down for a nap. "Did she really just go to sleep that easily for you?" The child had rubbed her eyes after she'd finished her bologna sandwich.

Kim gave her a look that was a mixture of pride and exhaustion. "Pretty much. Sophie is easy, but I think I deserve an easy one after the boys. I love them, and I don't know what I'd do without them, but they've certainly worn me out." She sipped her drink as she sat back down at the kitchen table. "I've been thinking about it a lot since you and I talked the other day, and I wonder what my life would've been like if I'd put my career ahead of my children."

Leona wasn't sure she cared for the phrasing, but she understood what her neighbor was trying to say. "And I've been thinking a lot, too. I wonder what I might be missing out on."

"I can fill you in on that. Late nights, long days, empty pockets. And a full heart." Kim smiled, although a bit sadly. "Plenty of arguments with the husband as to how to raise them, especially the boys. I don't think you'd have that problem with Hank, though."

Leona blinked, forgetting for a second that Hudson was Hank in the eyes of these people. Her face reddened as she remembered that he was also probably listening to every word they said. "No?"

"Oh, no. I've seen the way he looks at you." Kim smiled, shaking her finger teasingly at Leona. "He's not a man of many words, and I imagine he's not the sort to get mushy in front of strangers, but there's a certain look about him when he sees you from across the room."

The heat refused to leave her face as Leona swirled the olive in her glass. "I didn't realize."

"I noticed it a lot at the block party. He was finding chances to walk through the room to check on you, watching you from a distance just to make sure you were all right. It was adorable. You two act like you're still on your honeymoon."

Leona swallowed. Damn Hudson for insisting he listen to everything! But she had a role to play, and no one could blame her for doing that. "It often feels that way."

"Yes. It's like the two of you were destined to be together."

Kim's words made Leona's ears ring. Did she know? But how could she? And how was Hudson interpreting all this back at their makeshift headquarters if he had heard all this?

"Kevin and I felt the same, way back when." She glanced at the window, waxing reminiscent. "I wanted to be a doctor, though. Oh, I know. I don't seem like the type. But way back then, before I ever had any little ones, I still had plenty of brain cells. I wasn't too tired to think straight, and I loved the idea of studying the body. I thought it was so fascinating that we have these rules about how the body works, but in reality, we're all a little different, you know?" She turned her piercing green eyes to Leona.

"Sure, of course." Leona's phone had beeped,

and she excused herself for a second while she took it out to read the text message.

You've got to get home. Right now. It was from Hudson, of course.

She put the phone away. "Sorry about that. What were you saying?"

"Just that everyone is a little different. People like you and I are different, I think. And Hank." Kim's fingers fiddled nervously with the stem of her martini glass.

Leona carefully controlled her facial features, not wanting to give anything away, but it was clear that Kim knew something. "What do you mean?"

Her hostess let out a light, nervous laugh. "I shouldn't beat around the bush so much. I'm sorry. What I'm really trying to say is that I know what the two of you are."

If that was true, then it was damn strange for her to be so calm about it. Leona knew something was off here. "And what's that?"

"Lion shifters, of course!" Kim burst out laughing, fanning her face as she blinked back tears. "Oh, I'm so glad to finally get that out. I could tell right away. Takes one to know one, right? And I understand why you wouldn't want to talk about it. It's the sort of thing that not everyone accepts, and who could blame them?"

Leona let out a laugh herself, mostly just because she didn't know what else to do. No one at the block party had mentioned anything about the local pride or the fact that anyone was a shifter, and it was starting to make her wonder if they were watching the right group of people at all. "Right. Of course."

"I wanted to talk to you about joining our pride, dear. You can never surround yourself with too many good people, and I think the two of you are just about the cream of the crop." Kim beamed as she poured them each another drink.

Leona knew she was treading on dangerous territory. Kim could be genuine, but she could also be setting her up. It didn't help that her phone continued going off.

Seriously. I need to talk to you.

Leona.

Hudson would just have to wait. There were bigger things happening here. She turned back to Kim. "Have you talked to anyone else in your pride about this? What does your husband think?"

Kim waved away those worries as she sat back down. "They're all for it! I mean, I haven't talked to everyone as an entire group. We haven't had a meeting in a while. Everyone's been so busy. But that's life for you! And I have no doubt the two of you would be voted in. I mean, you're part of the neighborhood!" She leaned back in her chair and sipped her martini happily, looking quite proud of herself for inviting new members to join them. "It's as simple as getting everyone together, which I've been planning to do anyway."

Before Leona could respond, a small face with wide eyes peeked out from the hallway. Sophie's hair, almost as bright red as her mother's, was rumpled and she knuckled the corner of her eye. "I don't want to go to sleep anymore."

Kim's shoulders sagged in defeat, but she winked at Leona. "I guess I spoke too soon about that one, didn't I?"

But Sophie looked up at Leona and grinned. "You're still here?" She raced across the kitchen and launched herself into Leona's lap. "I thought you'd be gone."

Leona pulled her up, enjoying the warm softness of the little body against her. Sophie had to be about three or four, old enough to talk and interact, but still young enough to be completely endearing. "No, I haven't left yet. I'll have to soon, though."

"But I want you to play with me! Do you like Barbies?"

Leona laughed despite herself. It was just too damn cute. There was so much going on in the room, and this innocent child had no idea. Leona had never been much of one to play with Barbies, but she wasn't about to hurt the kid's feelings. "Barbies are fun. And so are trucks."

"You play with trucks?" Sophie's brows burrowed down over her eyes as she pulled back to look Leona in the face. "Those are boy toys!"

"That's not necessarily true. My brother always had trucks, soldiers, and dinosaurs, and I played with all of them." She remembered those days with Steve, when the two of them would be crouched on the living room carpet pretending to blow each other up while Tracy looked on in disgust. It was the best.

"Girls are supposed to play with Barbies and babies and play house," Sophie insisted.

Leona knew it wasn't her job to teach someone else's child what they should and shouldn't play with and how gender roles played a part in life, but she desperately wished she could tell this little girl about everything she'd done as a soldier. She could just imagine what Sophie would do when she found out

Leona had jumped out of helicopters and used explosives. That would have to wait; more likely, it would probably never happen. If she gave away her past now, Kim might change her mind entirely. Leona and Hudson had a good opportunity to officially join the local pride that Kim and Kevin belonged to, and they knew that was the one that was causing trouble.

"Sophie, dear, don't bother our guest," Kim admonished gently.

"She's not bothering me," Leona insisted, giving the girl a hug before setting her down on the floor. "I do have to get going, though. I've got some things I need to do this afternoon." She headed toward the door, and Sophie insisted on holding her hand.

Kim cleared her throat. "I do hope you'll think about what I said. I know we kind of got interrupted, and I apologize for that, but I think it would be good for you. You know, definitely knowing you belong here."

Leona nodded, trying to read Kim's face. She looked so genuine. If the pride was involved in trafficking illegal weapons, then why would they want any new members? It would be a risk, since they wouldn't know if those new neighbors could be trusted to keep a secret. The only thing that truly made sense was that they'd somehow discovered Leona and Hudson were there to take down their operations, and this was their way of luring the outsiders into a trap. But it was hard to imagine Kim as capable of such a thing. There was only one way to find out.

"I'll definitely think about it. And of course, I'll have to talk to Hank about it." He'd be interested to hear this new turn of events, even if he was pissed at her for not responding to his texts.

"Will you come back soon?" Sophie asked pitifully, rubbing her eye once again. The poor thing really was tired, she just didn't want to miss out on any of the excitement. She clutched a little harder at Leona's hand.

Leona crouched down next to her. For the most part, her hope of gathering intelligence during this outing hadn't gone as she'd planned at all. She'd been thrust into a woman's world, where conversation could only be about raising children and reminiscing over the past, with a few recipes sprinkled in. It was frustrating to know that she couldn't infiltrate suburban America the same way she could third-world countries.

But now that Kim had invited them into the fold, she had every reason to come back. Plus, she was starting to like her neighbors. "I'll have to see what I can do about that. I had a nice time hanging out with you, though."

Sophie threw her arms around Leona's neck. "I like you, and I don't want you to go!"

"Sophie, dear, that's very sweet, but she said she's got to go. You're going to have to let go." Kim opened the door to prove her point and gasped.

Leona looked up to find Hudson standing on the threshold, his fist raised as he was about to knock.

10

Hudson dropped his hand and forced a smile as he looked at Kim. "Sorry to startle you."

"No, that's all right!" the woman laughed. "Come on in."

"I was actually just coming over to let Leona know we've got to go. A bit of a family emergency, you see." That was the understatement—or perhaps the misstatement—of the year.

Leona shot him a secret glare before she turned her face back to the child, soft and sweet. "I promise I'll find a time to come and visit you again soon, okay? But you'll have to let me go so I can come back."

The little girl dropped her arms from Leona's neck, heavy with regret. "Okay."

"I've never seen her get so attached to someone so quickly," Kim said, her voice a mixture of apology and awe. "She's crazy about you."

"I'm pretty crazy about the little munchkin, too. Thank you so much for lunch, Kim. It was nice."

Hudson tried not to huff impatiently, but this was taking far too long.

"I'll give you a shout next week and maybe we can do it again! And," Kim paused, giving a meaningful look to Leona, "make sure you talk to your husband, okay?"

"I will." Leona gave Kim's arm a friendly squeeze and walked out the door. She kept the smile on her face until the front door closed behind them and they were down the porch steps. "What the hell are you doing coming over here and retrieving me like that? I'm perfectly capable of getting home myself, you know."

"Clearly not, considering you completely ignored my messages." Hudson reached out to take her by the elbow, but she snatched her arm away. "Did you even read them?"

"Of course, I did. But I had my own important things going on over there." They'd turned out onto the sidewalk and toward their house, and Leona picked up the pace.

He lengthened his stride to keep up with her. "As important as discovering that their buyer is working with a known terrorist organization?"

Her steps faltered for a second, but then she charged on, crossing the street and up the walkway in front of their house. "Are you shitting me?"

"I wish. I'd sent everything from the exchange by the river down to headquarters like we talked about. While you were drinking martinis and eating finger sandwiches, I got a match on the guy's face." Hudson punched his code into the electronic lock and opened the door, shutting and relocking it behind them once they were inside. "So maybe next time I tell you to get home, you'll listen to me."

"Nope." She whirled on him. "I'm not going to say that's not vital information, but I was making some interesting progress of my own."

He ran a hand through his hair, which was actually staying in place now that he had that hair gel Leona had bought for him. He had yet to thank her for it, but this wasn't the time. "Look, Leona, I respect you and everything you've done for our country, but I don't think you understand what we're supposed to be doing here. Making friends with the local housewives is only going to get us so far."

She stepped forward purposefully. Her makeup

was more subtle than what the other women in the neighborhood wore, but it accentuated her brown eyes and soft mouth. Even when she was scowling at him, she was gorgeous in her blouse and with her hair done up. "For your information, Hudson, I was doing a lot more than just sitting around chatting about house cleaning tips. Kim has officially invited us to join their pride."

The breath left his lungs and refused to come back in for a moment. "Well," he finally said, slowly, "it looks like we're both making progress then, aren't we?"

"Yes, we are. And I think it's about damn time you give me the credit I deserve. You don't know me, and you don't trust me. I get that to a certain extent, but I'm just as capable of getting out there and doing the job as you are. I'm sick and tired of tiptoeing around your fucking male ego because you have some ridiculous idea that you have to be the one in control." Her eyes flashed, and he recognized that elegant, steadfast lioness once again.

Hudson felt his own eyes darken as his breath came faster. He closed that small distance left between them. "And maybe I'm tired of you thinking you can just waltz out the door without me worrying about you, Leona. It doesn't matter how capable you are of taking care of yourself. I still want to protect you, to keep you safe from everything we're dealing with."

Leona had room to back away from him, but she refused. "Just because you feel that way doesn't give you the right to step in and take control of everything we do. I don't see how the two of us can continue to work together under these conditions."

"I think you're right." In an instant, he crushed his lips to hers, pressing their bodies together as he took her by the hips and pulled her forward. She stiffened for a moment before her lips softened, returning the kiss. Hudson groaned as he brought one hand up to touch her hair. He'd been thinking about this ever since he'd met the woman. It hadn't been all that long, and yet he felt as though he'd waited an eternity to touch her, as though his body had always known she was out there somewhere, waiting for him.

Her breath was soft and warm against his skin, and she fit so perfectly into his arms. Hudson immediately forgot about everything else they had going on. The fire he carried for her consumed him above all else as he deepened the kiss, feeling the sensation of his tongue against hers. It was her turn to let out a low moan, but then she splayed her hand against his chest and pulled back.

"Can we really do this?" she whispered breathlessly, her eyes shining up into his.

His embrace tightened around her. "We *need* to do this."

She nodded and kissed him again. Hudson's mind was completely gone. Every cell in his body lived only for this moment. He needed her as though he had an itch buried deep inside himself that only she could scratch. His fingers pulled at the delicate fabric of her blouse, removing it from the waistband of her pants so that he could touch the soft skin of her lower back. He let his hands rove upward over the smooth planes of her back and then around to cup her breasts through the thin fabric of her bra.

Leona's hands were working, too. She clutched at his t-shirt at first as though holding onto him for dear life, but as things progressed and she began to relax, she was exploring as well. She touched the delicate skin at the base of his throat where his pulse pounded and buried her fingers in his hair as their tongues entwined.

"I've needed you for so long," Hudson whispered as he pulled at the small buttons on the front of her shirt, exposing her inch by inch. "You're the most incredible woman I've ever met. You have no idea what you do to me." He backed her up toward the couch.

She surprised him by pushing him down onto the cushions and straddling his hardness. The strong muscles of her thighs touched his, turning him on all over again. "Oh, yes. I do."

He peeled away that blouse, such a thin and flimsy thing, yet it and the rest of her clothes had served as such a barrier between them. Her skin was smooth and tempting beneath it, and he wanted so badly to touch every inch of her that he almost didn't know where to begin. He ran his palms up her sides like a sculptor testing marble, delighting in the way every muscle and bone underneath was arranged. "I only wanted to protect you so much because I care about you."

Leona leaned forward, pressing her lips to his and then trailing her kisses down the side of his neck. She easily undid the button and zipper of his jeans and pushed them down off his hips. "I know."

He could have argued with her on that point, but any interest in doing so was zapped out of his body by the thought of their skin actually touching. She had him out of his jeans and his boxers now, and it was time he returned the favor. The tiny buttons of her slacks were a challenge for his eager fingers, but he was rewarded for his work with the sight of her in pale pink panties that matched her bra.

Hudson was enticed by the glimpse of her nipples under the fabric of her bra. He pulled her down onto his lap and kissed first one and then the other gently, his excitement continuing to build as he pulled her breast into his mouth, his tongue lingering on each nipple through the soft fabric until he left it wet and warm in his wake before moving to the other one. Leona shivered and wriggled against him as he worked. "Do you like that?" he whispered against her before sucking her back into his mouth again.

"Yes," she panted, throwing her head back. She was growing warm between her legs where she was pressed against his erection, and Hudson squeezed her backside.

"What do you want?" he teased. He knew exactly what he wanted, and it was hard to imagine she wanted anything different. But Hudson wanted to hear it from her, hear those words straight from her lips and into his bloodstream, so that neither one of them would need to question what they were doing. "Tell me what you want, Leona."

She shivered again, the silky fabric setting his

skin on fire. "I want *you*, Hudson. I've wanted you all along."

That was all he needed. Hudson tore at her underwear, the fine material dissolving in his grasp as he tore it apart with a low growl. He buried himself inside her as he worked at the clasp of her bra, releasing her glorious breasts so that he could see them in their full beauty. He suckled and kissed them again, tasting the warm skin without the garment between them any longer.

Leona moaned as she thrust and ground her hips against him, moving in time to his own drive as he plunged inside her. The heat of her was almost too much to bear, and yet he never wanted this to end. It was the middle of the afternoon, and he was making love to his coworker in the living room of their base of operations, but he only cared about the way they felt against each other.

"God," he whispered as he felt her thighs tighten around him. "Tell me how you like it, Leona. I'll give you anything you want." His hands roved up to tangle in her hair as he angled her mouth down for another kiss. His excitement built as he felt himself inside her in both places, sinking into her heat.

"This," she whispered back when they came up for air. "Just this."

"I want to make you come." He wanted to see what she looked like when she let go, when she wasn't putting up those stone walls she kept around herself all the time, when she was truly just herself.

"Oh, you are." She clenched around him as her abdomen sucked inward, and he felt the energy winding up inside her. His own body responded in kind, tightening and surging as she began shivering around him. Those shivers turned to full-on convulsions as he gripped her hips and pulled her down hard onto him. Leona let loose a wild cry as she took what she needed, her nails burying into his shoulders and her head whipping from side to side.

Hudson was right after her, tipped over the edge by Leona's pleasure. He felt the way they moved together inside her. There was no going back, and he didn't want to. He had everything he needed right there in his arms, and his body flooded with ecstasy as he filled her. Hudson gripped at her hips, feeling everything that had built up between the two of them over the past week finally exploding. He pressed his forehead against her shoulder, panting.

11

Leona woke the next morning. Her entire body felt extremely heavy, but in the most pleasant way possible. Hudson lay next to her in the big bed, and she gently touched the strong muscles of his arm as he slept.

She could almost laugh out loud at how much things had changed between them in the matter of a few minutes. No, that wasn't really true. Things hadn't exactly changed; it was just that they'd both finally let themselves admit what they had between them.

After they'd had sex on the couch, they tried to return to work. Hudson muttered some sort of excuse about tracking the weapons that Kevin and Sean had sold, and Leona had returned with the fact that they needed to decide what to do about Kim's invitation. But as soon as they'd enclosed themselves in the guest room that also served as a workspace, they couldn't keep their hands off each other. They'd wound up in the big bed in the master bedroom, where they'd thoroughly explored each other's bodies once again.

Leona bit her lip as she watched him sleep. He was a formidable man, and even when slumbering, he looked like he was ready for action. His strong muscles, wide chest, and solid jaw would be intimidating to anyone who knew what he was capable of doing as a soldier. But she'd seen him in action in the bedroom, and Leona also knew just how gentle and attentive he could be. Hudson was a generous lover. He seemed more concerned that she get what she needed out of the exchange than having his own needs met, although that wasn't a problem, either. He knew just when to hold her softly and when to tighten his grip. His commanding attitude could be annoying when they were simply trying to live and work together, but it turned her on in bed.

She smiled, tempted to wake him up for another round. But no matter how they felt about each other and how good their bodies felt when they worked in unison, they had other work to do. She rolled toward the edge of the bed.

A hand locked around her wrist with an iron grip and yanked her back so that she was sprawled out on his chest, her hair falling all over both of them. "Just where do you think you're going?" Hudson asked, one eye open.

"To work," she replied, although feeling her bare breasts against his skin was giving her second thoughts. "And to the kitchen for some coffee, I think."

He sighed. "Coffee is fine, but I think I have to call in sick today."

A crease formed between her brows. "Are you not feeling well?"

"Oh, I feel fine. I just want to stay in bed all day." Hudson grabbed her other arm and pulled her further over so that she straddled him.

"That sounds wonderful, but as I recall, we each had some startling revelations we needed to explore." Leona was tempted to spend just a little more time between the sheets with him, but then there was no telling when they'd actually be able to stop. "Let's get that coffee."

He sighed and let her go, sitting up and dumping her onto the mattress next to him with a laugh. "I guess you're right. After all, if this pride is dealing with terrorists, we've got a bigger mess on our hands that we realized." Hudson kissed her shoulder before launching off the other side of the bed and looking for his clothes.

"That's true," she admitted, trying to put herself back in the right mindset to handle the mission. "And I've got to get back to Kim on her offer of joining the pride. It's the perfect opportunity to learn what's really happening and what their motivations are. I wonder if they even realize what they're doing. Anyway, I thought I'd call her up and arrange another lunch date."

"Too dangerous." Hudson pulled on his jeans and zipped them, his abs rippling as he reached for a shirt. "You can't go back over there alone."

Leona frowned at him, and for the first time since they'd returned to the house, she began to doubt what they'd just done. Somehow, she had imagined that their physical attraction would lead to a mutual understanding of each other; that they'd no longer need to argue about how to continue this mission. "Hudson, don't be like that."

"Be like what?" He paused to look at her, with his arms in the sleeves of his shirt before he'd pulled it over his head.

"Overprotective. This is part of the mission, and I'm making good progress."

He had visibly stiffened. "I explained to you why I feel that way. I thought you understood."

She thought she had, too, but in a different way. "Yes, but it's different when we're just being us and when we're part of the Force." Leona paused, not liking the thoughts that were creeping through her mind. "Hudson, you didn't sleep with me just to get your way, did you?"

"What?" The mattress dipped and he was next to her, the t-shirt he'd grabbed balled between his hands. "Look at me."

She turned her face up toward him uncertainly. Leona had never felt unsure about anything in her life. She'd always known exactly what she wanted and how to get it, and she'd never shied away from hard work or difficult situations. But there was something about Hudson—especially now that they'd dealt with the sexual tension that had been looming between them—that made her question things she'd never thought to dispute before. "Yeah?"

"Don't think that for a second," Hudson soothed, reaching up to brush a strand of her hair back from her face. "What happened, what we did together, didn't have anything to do with the mission or the

Force. It was something we'd been avoiding since we met, but there's no point in doing that anymore."

"Okay." She felt somewhat mollified by his words. Hudson hadn't lied to her, and she could see the authenticity in his eyes. He was right, of course, and she was just allowing herself to be a silly girl. If Hudson had any thoughts of manipulating her through her body, he could've done it when they'd first arrived instead of waiting.

"If we've taken care of that, then I guess we need to take care of the other elephant in the room." He leaned forward, resting his elbows on his knees and running his hands through his hair.

Leona studied his wide back, noting the strength of it. Though there were very little similarities between his human body and his feline one, she swore she could see similar outlines of muscles and the same stretch of his spine. He was beautiful. "What's that?"

He looked at her over his shoulder. "That we're meant to be together."

"Fated." The word fell from her lips unbidden, though it'd been lurking in the back of her mind ever since that day when she'd shown up at the Force's headquarters and Hudson had flung the door open. She'd known it in that moment as a deep and primal instinct, one that didn't fit in with modern society and logic and yet that was undeniably true. "I know. Is that a problem?"

He rose from the bed and crossed the room, turning around to lean against the dresser. "I don't want to sound like a complete ass and say yes. I mean, we both know how this works. I imagine you grew up the same way I did, with your parents and grandparents talking about how important it is to find the one person you're meant to be with; being told never to settle for anything less because it won't be right."

Leona nodded. She had been told such things, though they'd never played a prime role in her thoughts. It was an idea for a far, far distant future, one that might never even happen. Her life was all about her career and her country, and fate had a different role in that. "So you're saying it *is* a problem."

Hudson sighed and looked down for a moment before he met her eyes again. "If things were different, then no. I mean, I'm a man and I'm a lion. I've been restless and shifty, knowing something's been missing. I think on some level I knew it was a mate. There's something nice about the idea of coming home to someone who understands you and wants to be with you. Then, you can always look at it from a business standpoint," he continued, holding out his hand as though he were looking at a tiny world that fit in his palm. "I'm the head of a large company that's making important strides in the world. How amazing would it be to have someone at my side, someone who has a good work ethic, who's seen what things are like beyond the borders. Someone who's not just after me for my money. If that was how things were, then I'd take you back to my apartment in D.C. and never let you leave."

She could see that feral urge in his eyes, and she had to admit she liked it, but there was much more he wasn't saying. "Just tell me, Hudson. Don't toy with me."

"I'm not trying to. It's just that things with the Force changed a bit when you showed up looking for a job. It had never been anyone but just us guys, and now there's a drop dead gorgeous woman in the mix. We all agreed that none of us would get involved with you." His expression was soft and regretful as he studied her.

"Oh. Oh, I see." She'd thought he was just trying to find some nice way to say he really wasn't interested in being committed right now, but thanks for all the hot sex anyway. No, this was completely different. "If we get involved, then I lose my spot on the Force." She cursed softly under her breath, wishing she hadn't been so stupid to let her heart rule her head in that moment of passion.

"Or we *both* do." He slowly put his shirt on now, careless of the wrinkles he'd put into it by holding it so tightly.

"Why didn't you tell me earlier? We could've avoided this." Her mind flashed back to the way they'd held each other, the way his hands had pulled at her, the way his mouth felt against hers. It felt so right and so good, and even now she couldn't say with absolute certainty whether or not she'd have stopped herself if she'd known the truth. Regardless, she liked to have all the facts before making any decision.

Hudson gave a short, sarcastic bark of laughter as he took a pair of socks out of the dresser drawer. "How many reasons would you like me to list? Maybe it was because I was foolish enough to think I could control myself around you. Or maybe it was because I was in denial about actually meeting my mate. Or maybe..." He turned and launched himself at the bed.

The next thing Leona knew, he was on top of her. His hands were on either side of her, his legs straddling hers, pinning her into place. He's pounced on her like the giant cat he was, and she wasn't interested in fighting him off.

"Maybe," he continued, "I was secretly hoping it wouldn't matter, because you're so fucking irresistable and I knew I'd never be able to keep my paws off you." He kissed her softly and then stood, adjusting his pants that now had a lot less room between the legs. "You make it very difficult to concentrate, Sergeant Kirk."

"I'll take that as a compliment." She studied him for a long moment, wishing she knew what the right decision was. "In the meantime, though, we do have a job to do. I don't want to just cancel it all, not now that we're finally starting to figure things out here. I say we just don't say anything at all for now. We can worry about it when we get back to headquarters." It would be awkward, and there was a good chance she'd find herself looking for another job, but it didn't make sense to just stop now.

For a moment, he looked like he was going to argue with her, but he bobbed his head. His solemn expression then turned to a grin. "I guess that'll only help our cover, since I'm always gazing at you from across the room."

"You *were* listening!" She picked up a pillow and tossed it at him.

"Only checking in every now and then to make sure you were safe. After all, you were right. There was no point in both of us listening to the same conversation when I could be monitoring other channels. And, of course, getting the information on the real identity of the buyer." He tossed the pillow back on the bed.

"Hang on." Leona realized she was still sitting there completely naked while talking about the operations. "I'm going to take a shower and you can make the coffee. Then we can talk."

"Yes, ma'am," he said with a mock salute before heading toward the kitchen.

A hot shower was just what she needed to clear her head. Leona knew she had to remember no matter how good-looking Hudson was or how much influence their entwined destinies had on her, there was still plenty of work to be done. She inhaled the steam as she lathered up her body, smiling to herself as she remembered just how much Hudson had appreciated every curve. No, damn it! That was just going to get her distracted again.

When she got out, Leona threw on a t-shirt and a pair of jeans, leaving her hair down to air dry. She followed the scent of coffee into the kitchen, where Hudson was also laying plates heavy with food on the table.

"I figured you'd be hungry," he said, looking a little sheepish. "I know I am. We sort of skipped dinner last night."

She sat down to the meal, realizing he was right. They'd been so busy discovering the connection between them that they hadn't had a thought for food. "It's delicious. You cooked the bacon perfectly." He'd also made scrambled eggs, toast, and a fresh fruit salad. It might not have been the most complicated meal in the world, but it was exactly what she needed, and she planned to eat all of it. "Okay. So tell me more about this buyer."

Hudson sat across the table from her, sliding a tablet in her direction. He'd already pulled up a few pictures of the man they'd seen on the boat. "Our friend is Husam Simmons. He's been investigated several times for suspected terrorism, but so far, the U.S. government hasn't officially been able to nail him on anything other than a few traffic tickets and tax evasion."

"Interesting name," Leona mused. She finished with her bacon and tried the eggs. She couldn't identify what Hudson had used to season them, but they were scrumptious.

"Yes. Born in America, but there are some Middle Eastern influences throughout his family tree. I hate to say that profile unfortunately fits the bills of so many terrorists these days. And I couldn't find any evidence of his relatives causing trouble. My guess is that he's gotten involved with one of these training organizations that brainwashes them into believing they're doing the right thing by taking out some of his fellow citizens." Hudson frowned as he spread butter on a piece of toast. "They can shut down the borders and ban travelers from certain countries all they want, but it won't stop these guys."

Leona's chest clenched a little. It had always been a risky business to work overseas with the Army. She'd been involved in operations that she knew the military wouldn't make public for decades, and even once they did, people still probably wouldn't believe what had happened. But it was entirely different when it was happening on their own turf, right next to happy suburban families and their children. Children like Sophie. "So what, exactly, do you think this guy is doing with these weapons?"

"I think he's planning a major attack of some

sort. I don't know exactly when or where, but I do know that Garrison has been tracking him ever since he gave me the report of the facial match. He's stored everything in a rented facility further down the river in Southern Illinois. It's pretty rural down there, so he probably figures nobody will notice. Until he's ready to put on a show, that is." Hudson got up from the table to get the jelly out of fridge.

"Interesting." Leona was glad to know that their comrades were keeping an eye on this guy. The two of them hadn't had a chance to follow Husam after he'd bought the weapons from Kevin and Sean, especially once they knew his reinforcements were so close by. "Any more detailed information about who he might be working with?"

"I've still got some connections with the Department of Homeland Security, so I'm waiting to hear back on that. In the meantime, we've tipped off the right authorities. If they do their job, Simmons won't have a chance to use those weapons." He put the lid back on the jelly and passed it across the table in case she wanted it.

Leona was happy with all the protein, but a little sugar didn't hurt, either. She absently topped her toast as she continued to scan the limited information on the tablet. "I wonder if our locals have any idea just who they're dealing with. From the reports we went over back at Headquarters, I understood they were just selling this stuff on the streets. I bet they'd shit their pants if they found out the truth."

"Fortunately, no one here is turning up on any lists. That makes me feel a little better about their intentions." He finished his breakfast and took his plate to the sink.

"Well, we might get the chance we need to find out." Leona almost wished there was more food, even though she didn't need to get too full. It was just so good, and Hudson had really helped her work up an appetite. "Kim wants us to join their pride. She said she'll just have to arrange a club meeting so everyone can vote on it."

Hudson finished rinsing his plate and poured a second cup of coffee. "Did she say if everyone in the neighborhood is part of the pride? I got the impression it was otherwise when we went to that block party."

Leona shook her head. "Not specifically, but she did mention that not everyone was like us. At first, I thought we were outed. She just meant lion shifters." Kim seemed like such an innocent woman, and Leona had to wonder if she had any idea what her husband was up to when he left the house in the middle of the night.

"When will this meeting take place?"

"I imagine sometime after I give her our answer. I'm supposed to discuss our membership with my 'husband' and get back to her. Which brings me back to going to her place for lunch today if she's available." She looked at him over her coffee cup and raised one eyebrow, affecting a snobby accent. "I don't know, darling. Do you think we'll settle in this area permanently? Should we join their little club, or should we aim our sights a little higher? Say one of the country clubs closer to St. Louis?" They shared a laugh over the joke.

"Call her up," Hudson said resignedly, "and let me know what I'm supposed to wear to this meeting."

12

"You're quiet this evening." Leona was standing in front of the dresser, watching in the mirror as she put on a pair of dainty earrings that went nicely with the white jeans and blue sleeveless top she'd picked up at the mall that day.

They'd both needed to go shopping, in fact, because they hadn't brought quite enough clothing for all these social events. Hudson grunted as a response to her question as he slid into the pale yellow button-down. He didn't really like it, but it seemed like the sort of thing that was right for the event.

"Have the guys come up with anything else on Simmons?" She adjusted her hair before stepping out and across the hall for a pair of shoes, returning in just a few seconds. Leona had started sleeping in the master bedroom with him, but she hadn't moved all her belongings over there yet.

It was an arrangement that Hudson felt suited them both, since they enjoyed each other's company so much and were yet uncertain about what the future would hold for their relationship. "He's laying low for the moment. Garrison called a while ago, all pissed off because the local authorities weren't doing anything to raid the rented storage unit. I guess they don't think something like that can happen in their little part of the world."

"We know it can happen anywhere, but not everyone has witnessed it like we have."

He grunted again.

"Okay, seriously." Leona stood in front of him now, her hands on her hips. "What's the problem? I wouldn't bug you like this, but we're getting ready to go into a pretty uncertain situation. If there's something on your mind, I'd rather know about it now instead of later."

He met her gaze, trying to decide how much he should tell her. There were so many thoughts going through his head, so many things to think about. He'd been on plenty of missions, both with the Army and with the Force, and he'd always been able to stay out of his own head. But there was never a woman like Leona with him, a woman that he knew he had to protect at all costs. They were a good pair, and he wouldn't have asked for anyone else to go with him into the field, but it still made it more difficult. If it were Drake or Flint or Garrison, there would be no questions.

Drake, Flint, and Garrison, however, were part of the problem. Hudson had seriously considered calling a couple of them in to serve as backups just in case things went south while they were at this meeting. But having them there also meant he might have to tell them what was going on between himself and Leona, and he wasn't ready for that. He wasn't ready for them to make a democratic decision to pull one or both of them out of Illinois and go a different route.

He also didn't want to bring that up to Leona. He knew keeping their secret was just as much of an issue for her as it was for him, and it wasn't fair to throw it back in her face yet again. Still, he had to answer. "I'm just not certain about this. Don't make that face; I'm not saying I won't go or that we shouldn't go. It just makes me a little apprehensive since we have proof that these people are involved in illegal affairs."

"You don't strike me as the type who gets nervous." She said it calmly and earnestly, not critically.

"Not normally," he admitted. "There's just more on the line this time. Let's go." He led the way out to the garage.

The drive out to the clubhouse that Kim had given Leona the address to was a quiet one. The two of them had already gone over their plan. They each had a pistol concealed in their clothing—a small measure that Flint would no doubt smirk at—and a small recording device. Whatever happened, they needed proof of it. But they'd already gone over everything, and there was little else to talk about.

"This looks like the place," Hudson said as he pulled up in front of a large house out by the lake. The road to get to it had been a dark and lonely one, but the double wraparound porches of the clubhouse were blazing with light. More lights lined the asphalt driveway that brought them up to a sizable parking area. Quite a few cars were already there, and they'd arrived fifteen minutes early. The rest of the pride must have been eager for things to begin.

"Make sure you stay in character," Hudson muttered as he put the car in park and turned off the ignition.

"No shit."

Hudson got out and took her arm as they walked toward the front door. "And no matter what happens, we can't become part of their pride. We can't risk them getting inside our heads and finding out more information than what we're willing to give them. It would mean putting the rest of the Force in danger, not just ourselves."

"I know."

He paused at the door, her hand still tucked in his elbow, and turned to her. "Leona, no matter what happens in here—"

"It'll be fine," she said with a smile. "I know it will. Let's do this."

Hudson nodded, knowing he'd been ridiculous to worry so much. Yes, he was doing this big step of their mission with the woman he was fated to—and loved—but there was no one else in the universe he'd rather be with. He knocked on the door.

It swung open almost instantly. "Here you are!" Kim squealed with delight as she ushered them in. "I'm so glad you came! Everyone was very excited to get together. Come on in! Kevin's here, and Sean, and everyone else! Not Cathy, though." She whispered this last part in Leona's ear with a giggle.

The clubhouse was slightly outdated, but nice.

Hudson surveyed the room, noting all of the available exits. He knew Leona would be doing the same, but old habits died hard. He shook Kevin's hand heartily when he came forward.

"Nice to see you again, Hank! Come on in and grab a plate. We've got a good old-fashioned buffet going. I hope you like fried chicken."

"Of course."

The next hour or so passed by quickly and without incident. Hudson was introduced to several members of the pride that he hadn't met at the block party. There was plenty of food and drink passed around, and he stayed fully aware of just how much he consumed. The potted plant near the couch was more drunk at the end of the evening than he was. He hoped the alcohol would influence Kevin to admit what he'd been doing, but he had no luck in that area. Hudson tried to stay as close to Leona as possible, but the women had a habit of sweeping her out of the room.

Just when he was beginning to think it was going to be an uneventful evening, Kevin tapped a fork against his wine glass. "Ladies and gentlemen, if I could have your attention, please." The buzz of the crowd died down as everyone turned to him. Leona appeared out of nowhere and took Hudson's arm.

"We all know why we're gathered here tonight. We have new friends in the neighborhood, good people who we know would make a wonderful addition to our pride: Hank and Leona Talbott!"

The attendees all cheered and applauded. Hudson gave a small wave. He expected this to be a big deal, but he didn't like having all the attention turned on them.

"Hank, Leona," Kevin continued, "we'd like to officially invite you to become one of us. We're all here in your honor, and we'd be extremely privileged to induct you tonight."

"That's very kind of you," Hudson said, wondering just how he was going to get out of this without offending anyone. A request like this wasn't one the pride would've taken lightly, after all. "Leona and I have been discussing this wonderful opportunity almost constantly. It's an incredible honor, and I can't tell you how flattered we are that you would extend your circle to include us when you've known us for such a short amount of time."

Leona nodded and smiled at his side, but he could detect the waves of anxiety that radiated from her.

"That being said, I'm afraid we can't accept tonight." A heavy silence filled the room, and

Hudson could feel the suspicion rising. "You see, my wife isn't feeling all that well, and I really do need to get her home." He felt Leona slump a little against him. Nothing overly dramatic, but just enough to make his story seem feasible.

Kevin frowned. "I don't think you understand. This isn't an option. We can't just have you accept an invitation into the fold and then reject it."

"Not rejecting, just postponing," Hudson corrected softly. "If you'll excuse us, we'll get on home. Then we can meet up with you another time and get this done." He moved toward the door, bringing Leona with him.

"No." Kevin made a small gesture, and the other male members of the pride closed in around them. One, whom Hudson recognized as Chris, reached out to grab him. He blocked him easily enough, swinging his arm to the side, but not before another shifter had snatched Leona.

His momentary panic didn't last long. He hadn't yet seen her combat, but she could hold her own. Leona thrust her elbows back into the man's gut, then rammed her head back as he bent forward, sending him reeling away with a bloody nose.

"Dear, we don't need to make such a show of this," Kim said. She'd come up next to her husband, her glow of excitement replaced by worry. "We can do it another time. I don't mind putting another meeting together."

Kevin glared at his wife. "Stay out of this. We've got business to take care of."

Hudson felt his inner lion awaken at the threat of the crowd around him, and he was tempted to shift right then and there. But someone attacked him from behind, throwing him forward. Hudson stumbled, grabbing someone else nearby for balance. His shirt must have lifted at just the wrong angle.

"He's got a gun!"

Someone snatched it from the back of his waistband, but Hudson wasn't ready to give up the fight yet. More men fell on him, pinning his arms and taking him to the floor. He fought back, but there was only so much one man could do when he was so outnumbered. He heard Leona's grunts as she was experiencing the same, and the shriek of indignance as someone discovered she was armed as well.

Something thumped the back of his head and the world went dark.

HIS HEAD THROBBED as he peeled his eyes open. His

stomach churned, but he clenched his teeth against it as he tried to take in his surroundings. They'd thrown them in a room that looked like some sort of storage area with concrete walls and a solid door. There weren't any windows, and he could easily surmise they were in a basement. A single bulb burned overhead.

Leona's weight was heavy against his shoulder. Hudson instinctively reached out to check her for injuries, but his hands were bound. "Leona. Wake up."

She stirred, her head lolling to the side. Her eyes opened partway, making her look even more cranky than she normally did when she woke up in the morning. "What the hell happened?"

"Do you remember anything from upstairs?" he asked. Hudson could remember it far too clearly, but he knew they needed to keep talking. It would help them regain consciousness, and they needed to get clear-headed if they were going to get out of this.

"Shit. Yeah. I think so. I just can't believe they turned on us that fast." She experimented with the ropes at her wrists and made a face of disgust at them before lifting her foot and peeling off her shoe. A small folding knife fell to the floor.

"Clever girl," Hudson said proudly as he picked

it up. The blade was sharp, and he sliced through the rope easily before handing the knife to Leona so she could return the favor. "I knew there was a chance this could go badly, but I didn't think they'd react so harshly."

"That must mean they either know who we really are, or they're afraid we've found out who *they* are. How long have we been down here?"

Hudson automatically reached for his cell phone, but it was gone. Not a surprise. "No telling. Doesn't feel very long."

Leona got to her feet slowly, stretching her muscles and assessing her body. It looked like a waste of time, but Hudson understood what she was doing. She had to figure out just what she was capable of before she attempted an escape. "Have you looked at the lock yet?"

"I just woke up." He followed her to the door. The small hole in the simple handle indicated a typical indoor lock. "Interesting that they'd have the knob on that way. I'd guess that means they had someone in here before, but it must not have been anyone who knew what they were doing."

She was busy checking out the rest of the door. "It might not have been that at all. I've seen locking knobs on rooms like this before, just because that was what was available. Given how inept they seem at this weapons trafficking ordeal, I'd guess they weren't quite prepared for this."

"Made them paranoid enough not to want to let us go, though," Hudson remarked. "We either need something long and slim to undo the lock, or something we can pry the hinges off with."

"Yeah." Leona's response was absent-minded as she tilted her head at the door. "You think you can break this down? Maybe in your other form?"

"Possibly, but I'd rather not give them a heads-up that we're getting out when they hear me crashing against the wood. Better to sneak out if possible. Help me look." He turned to the shelves that took up two of the walls of the room and began sorting through boxes of old Christmas decorations.

She joined him, systematically starting on the other end of the shelves and looking thoroughly through each container. "Did you hear the way the women reacted when things went down?"

"What do you mean?" He wasn't interested in the pride's dynamics at the moment, more absorbed with getting out of their makeshift prison than anything. His mind was constantly working through alternate plans. If they couldn't break down the door, they'd need to catch their opportunity when someone came to check on them. If they shifted and busted through the door that way, they'd need to be prepared for a flood of members to come rushing in to subdue them again. If they were taken down a second time, they might not simply be knocked unconscious the next time.

"I mean, they acted like they had no idea what was happening. Kim looked embarrassed at her husband's actions. It was the women who were so freaked out about us being armed. Most of them ran out of the room." She flung a string of heart-shaped decorative lights to the side.

"What's your point?"

"They don't know what the guys are doing. The men were quick enough to jump in and keep us from leaving, even though it was perfectly reasonable that we might not want to go through the induction tonight. My guess is that they understood their secret was on the line, but the ladies didn't have a clue."

Hudson stopped what he was doing to look at her. "Does it really even matter now? I mean, we know they're involved in illegal activities. We know they're supporting terrorism, even if they don't know it. And whether or not they admit it, guys are always looking for a fight. They were probably happy to jump in just because they never get the chance for that sort of action. Granted, it wasn't exactly a fair fight, but they won't think about that until tomorrow."

"I think it matters, because it means it's not the entire pride that's involved. Ah!" she held up a Christmas ornament hook in the older style that was essentially a piece of bent wire. Leona straightened it and took it to the door. She poked the wire into the hole in the brass knob, searching for the tiny release button.

Hudson wasn't about to walk out into the clubhouse with little more than a tiny knife to protect them. He returned to the boxes he'd gone through, taking out a steel section of hollow tubing that was used as the center support for an artificial Christmas tree. Bits of tinsel were still stuck to it as he braced it over his shoulder like a baseball bat.

The click of victory was loud in the concrete room. Leona looked at him over her shoulder to be sure he was ready before slowly turning the knob. She pressed her ear to the door, listening for anyone outside before easing it open.

They found themselves in a larger basement room. It was mostly dark, but the light over the stairs illuminated a man who'd been stationed on guard duty. He looked uncertain as he shifted his pistol from one hand to the other, glancing up the stairs frequently. Hudson cussed silently in his head. This man wasn't a trained soldier. He was someone who'd gotten caught up in something much bigger than himself, something he didn't know how to handle. But he was also someone who would alert the rest of the pride as soon as he realized something was wrong.

Hudson raced forward on silent feet, swinging the tree pole over his head and bringing it down hard on the man's skull. The dull thud vibrated through the metal as the guard fell. Leona caught him before he hit the floor and began dragging him backwards. Hudson understood what she was doing, and he joined her in stowing the unconscious man in the same storage closet they'd just escaped from. As extra security, Leona wrapped him in a length of garland that she tied expertly around his wrists and feet.

"Christmas in July," Hudson whispered with a smile. "Let's see what else we can find."

The clubhouse seemed eerily quiet at first, but he knew they wouldn't have just abandoned their prisoners and left them in the care of a solitary guard. The two of them slowly made their way up the stairs to the industrial kitchen, fully equipped with stainless steel counters and massive appliances. Like the basement, the light had been left on over the sink but the rest of it was dark.

Voices emanated from the common area where the party had been held. They were low and concerned. Hudson crouched near the doorway to listen with Leona right behind him.

"I don't like this, Kevin. We need to figure out what to do."

"I told you, I'm doing that!" the Alpha snapped. "I can't exactly work a miracle!"

"Everyone, just stay calm." This voice was Sean, and Hudson could easily imagine him in his Hawaiian shirt, gesturing downward with his palm to ease the assembly. "We've already taken one large step in explaining that the Talbotts were infiltrators from the other pride. As far as anyone knows, we acted against them for the safety of our own pride."

"I still say we should've let everyone know what we've been doing, and a long time ago, too. I know we agreed to keep the weapons a secret when we first got into this, thinking it was safer that way. But we're putting everyone's lives on the line and they don't even know it."

"No one's life is on the line," Kevin retorted.

"We've been making a shit ton of money on those weapons, money that we desperately needed. What the rest of them don't know won't hurt them. After all, they're not the ones making midnight deliveries."

Another worried voice piped up. "The Talbotts could be cops. Why else would they come in here with guns? And why would they refuse to join the pride?"

Sean let out a derisive laugh. "They're not cops. They had guns, but they didn't have any identification. Have you really ever seen a cop go anywhere without a badge? I don't think so."

"Then who are they?" the worried voice pressed. "And why would they come here?"

"Maybe you should ask my nosey wife who thinks it's her job to welcome everyone to the neighborhood and treat them like her new best friends. I don't fucking know!" Kevin was swiftly losing his temper, showing the side of him that had probably gotten him into this mess in the first place. "Damn it, I don't know who these people are. I don't know why they brought the guns in here or why they even agreed to come if they didn't want to be one of us. I also don't know why Kim had to invite them to begin with, so don't ask me."

"Well, you *did* tell her we needed to recruit more members," Sean commented.

The resulting noise that resounded from the room indicated he'd earned a smack for his honesty.

"Let's just go find out who they are," one of the unidentified voices suggested. "They can't do anything to us down there, and they're still outnumbered."

"Maybe we can take the woman out first and question her," another proposed.

Hudson glanced behind him. The room was dim, but he could see the determination on Leona's face when she nodded. They didn't need to shift to speak telepathically. She understood, and she was just as ready as he was. She slipped backwards into the darkness, away from the door.

Footsteps pounded closer. Hudson calculated their distance, knowing that timing was key. He gripped the tree pole in his hands and glanced at the kitchen. There room was too full, and if he shifted, his lion wouldn't have any space to move. The erstwhile decoration was his best bet.

He pounced when the first figure came through the doorway and reached for the light switch. He never got a chance to touch it as Hudson clouted him across the face with the pipe. The man reeled backwards, taking a secondary member down with him as he grabbed out for balance.

"*You!*" Kevin roared. He launched himself at Hudson, prepared for an assault from the steel tube. He blocked it with his hand and forearm and cast it away. The Alpha was more dangerous than he looked in his chinos and polo. He launched a series of punches to Hudson's face, several rights and a left. Hudson staggered back but caught the next uppercut and shoved the man backwards.

A strange sound entered Hudson's ears, and he turned just in time to see Leona on top of the counter. She ran down the length of it, her legs strong and quick, a knife flashing in her grip as she leapt off the end, just past the pot rack on the ceiling and onto Kevin's back. She buried the knife in his shoulder. Blood spurted out from the wound, soaking into his shirt as he sank toward the ground.

Sean took advantage of Hudson's distraction, crashing into him with a strong shoulder. Hudson retaliated, bringing his knee up between the other man's legs. A sharp crack sounded from somewhere, but Hudson didn't have time to register the noise for what it was. He felt the air leave Sean's lungs as he doubled forward in pain, leaving the perfect opportunity. Hudson grabbed his head and twisted. The snap sent him to the floor, dead.

When he looked up to find his next victim, Hudson saw the three remaining men near the fridge. One of them held a pistol—Hudson's pistol—at arm's length. Leona was on the floor near Kevin, and there was far more blood than what should've come from the Alpha's knife wound.

Red rage filled Hudson's eyes. He could no longer control his inner beast as he understood that someone had hurt his mate. His anger thundered from his chest, his skull cracking as his face formed a muzzle around his roar. He charged forward, his paws manifesting just as they hit the ground. He felt his claws scrape against the hard floor of the kitchen, heard the rush of his blood in his ears, noted the air rushing through the individual fibers of his mane as he tucked in and made his final leap.

The man's neck snapped in Hudson's jaws, sending the pistol falling to the ground. The other men didn't bother sticking around to continue the fight. It was over.

13

"There's more than enough evidence to get the guilty parties locked away for a long time," Drake said approvingly. He, Flint, and Garrison had arrived to help sort out the remains of the pride. "The two of you did a good job."

"Thank you," Leona replied, feeling a certain sense of relief at hearing him say that. She'd understood that Drake's opinion counted for a lot, and there were many parts of the mission that felt completely botched to her.

"They're going to need some help getting back on their feet now that Kevin is going to jail and Sean is dead," Hudson remarked from beside her. "Although honestly, I think a few of them are happy about it. It doesn't take a rocket scientist to know they didn't have the best leadership."

"I can think of a few that probably aren't happy," Leona murmured. She detached herself from the rest of the Force, where they'd gathered the remains of the pride at the clubhouse. Leona hated that the other shifters had to visit the scene of the crime like this, but it was the biggest place available to gather everyone together.

Kim was standing in the corner of the living room, not far from where her husband had stood just the night before and announced that the "Talbotts" would be joining them. She had her hands folded in front of her, her fingers nervously sliding over each other.

"Are you holding up okay?" Leona asked gently.

"I should ask you the same, since you were the one who got shot," she replied with a brittle smile.

She gestured vaguely at her shoulder, where the wound was already almost healed. "I've already had a leg blown off, so this is nothing." It might've been a much bigger deal if the shifter had been a better shot.

"I should've known you weren't just a typical woman," Kim said, her eyes flicking up to watch the soldiers organizing the remaining shifters. "Then again, I also should've known my husband was doing something illegal. I can't believe he was that stupid, and I can't believe I was so foolish."

"Don't be so hard on yourself," Leona advised. "It sounds like most of the pride had no idea, but it was all going to come out in the end. None of this was your fault."

"I like to think I'm going to believe that someday." Kim's fingers shook as she pressed them to her forehead. "It's just all so crazy."

"I know." Leona truly felt bad for the woman. "And I'm sorry that I deceived you. It was just part of my job, but I really did enjoy the time we spent together. Believe it or not, you helped me understand that maybe there's another side of me I haven't explored yet."

"I'm glad to hear that. And I'm going to miss you." Kim caught her up in a tight hug and then continued to clasp Leona's arms as they separated. "I have to ask you something."

"Of course."

"You and Hank—I mean, Hudson. The two of you really are mates, aren't you? I mean, if you're not, then you two deserve an Oscar." This time Kim's smile reached her eyes.

Leona opened her mouth to reply, but looked

over her shoulder at Hudson instead. He was conferring with Flint and looked every bit the soldier. He was all about the mission and his duty, as was she. They hadn't talked about it any further, but now that they'd be going back to D.C., they'd have to. "I don't really know," she finally responded. "We're going to have to figure that out."

"When you do, let me know. I really would like to keep in touch. Now, if you'll excuse me, I need to check in with my mother. She's watching the kids for me." Kim moved away from the crowd.

Leona returned to the man who'd been her partner for the last week and a half. Hudson looked up at her. "Everything is under control here. An unofficial vote is putting Kim in charge of the pride, although I don't think she knows it. I guess they're more interested in throwing block parties than in funding terrorism."

"Any word on that front?" Now that they'd gotten the pride sorted out, Leona was ready to tackle the next problem.

"All taken care of," Hudson assured her. "Drake lit a fire under a few asses, and Husam Simmons is being thoroughly interrogated by Homeland Security. He won't be bothering anyone, and I have a feeling that his arrest will lead to more information about whatever organizations he's been working with."

"I'm a little pissed about that myself," Flint remarked as he walked up. "I would've liked the chance to crack open that storage unit and see just what he had in there. Drake says you can get packed up, by the way. Everything's under control here, and the two of you look like shit."

"Thanks a lot," Leona said with a smile.

The drive back to their home was a long and quiet one, but for different reasons than it had been when they'd first come to that club meeting. They'd only been living in Edwardsville for a short time, and Leona had known from the very beginning that it was merely a temporary situation. The whole thing—the nice home, the furniture, the slow mornings sipping coffee—was all just a sham to serve the mission. Still, as Hudson parked in the driveway and then headed inside to begin packing, Leona knew it was going to be difficult to let go of.

"I guess you haven't said anything just yet," she remarked as she folded her clothes and put them in her suitcase. The dress from the block party went in first so she wouldn't have to look at it.

Hudson glanced up at her before getting his

socks out of the dresser drawer. "It's not solely my decision, you know."

She pursed her lips as she added several pairs of jeans to her case. "Are you saying we don't have to tell them?" Leona wasn't sure how she felt about that idea. It would mean she'd get to keep her job, but she assumed that would also mean that she and Hudson couldn't be together anymore. It was like she couldn't win no matter which route she took.

"No, I'm not saying that at all," he replied after a moment. "I'm just saying that I'm not the only one involved. It wouldn't be fair of me to run to Drake and the guys behind your back. We need to go to them together. It's the right thing to do." Hudson snapped a shirt down off a hanger, began to fold it, then balled it up and tossed it in a duffle bag.

"I guess." She felt tears burning at the backs of her eyes, which pissed her off. "I've only been on one mission, but I'm really going to miss this job. I thought it was so perfect for me."

He was at her side in an instant, gently grabbing her wrists and turning her around to face him. "You know, you don't have to work. I make plenty of money for both of us. We could find a way to make it work."

"It's a nice idea, but it's not reality. I *do* need to work, Hudson. It's not about money." She felt completely defeated and drained, and she couldn't see any way out of this where they could get everything they wanted. It just wasn't going to happen, and she was too tired to imagine fighting for it. They were fated, but that didn't mean they were destined to live happily ever after.

"You know we have to tell them, right?"

He looked so disappointed that she almost changed her mind. But Leona was a soldier. She had to stand by her decisions; there was no room in life for waffling. "Yeah, I know."

"I mean, we have a loyalty to them."

"I said I know." She didn't want to talk about it anymore. Yes, it was the right thing to do. But it was going to break her heart no matter what they did.

"So, overall, we can sum up that everything went as well as it possibly could," Drake concluded, closing out the report.

They were all seated in SOS HQ back in D.C., reviewing the mission. "How do you two feel about it?"

"It definitely wasn't what I expected," Leona

admitted, "and I'd probably change a few things if I could go back and do it again. But we got things taken care of, so I really can't complain."

Drake nodded. "I'd ask Hudson this next question privately, but I think it's only fair that you hear what the rest of us think. Hudson, how was it? Is she worthy of her position here on the Force?" His eyes flicked between the two of them expectantly.

Leona stiffened. This was it. This was the moment she'd lose the one thing that she'd thought would keep her life going after the military. She'd be stuck looking for satisfying work in the form of a desk job or a retail position, something that would make her completely miserable.

Hudson cleared his throat and ran a hand through his hair. "Yes, I do believe she's worthy of the position. She's dedicated, determined, and thorough. She doesn't back down from risk or danger, and she's good at blending in to make friends with the potential enemy."

Drake smiled. "Sounds like just what we need around here."

"There's one more thing." Hudson looked at Leona apologetically. She gave him the slightest nod. "She's also fated to me. I mean, we're fated to each other."

The doctor's lips tightened into a hard line, and he tapped his fingers at the table as he glanced at the other Force members and then back at Hudson and Leona. "You know, Hud, we discussed this. Getting involved with another member of the Force is strictly forbidden."

"I know that. We both do."

Leona could feel every muscle in her body filling with tension. She wanted to throw up. It was so unfair to lose her position with the Army just from one wrong step, and now she was losing her position with the Force over something she had absolutely no control over. "I know this is going to create a problem, Sir, so I'll turn in my resignation."

"Hold on a second." Drake's tone was a warning as he stared down his communications officer. "Hudson, I take it this means you've been involved with Sergeant Kirk. We discussed this, and you knew what the rules were. You chose to break them, and that's grounds for immediate dismissal."

"You can't do that!" Leona shot to her feet. "I already said I'd quit, and believe me, that's one of the last things in the world I want to do. I love being on the Force, but it's only been part of my life for a short time. It's not the same for him!"

"Leona, stop," Hudson said gently as he pulled

her back into her seat. "He's right. I knew this was possible. It'll be all right."

But it didn't seem all right to her at all. It was bad enough that she should be denied her dream, but to do that to both of them? Leona could feel the anger and resentment building inside her and tried to figure out just what she was going to do with it. "Listen, Drake—"

"Hold on." He held out his hand, waving at her to calm down. "Before you get too bent out of shape, I should tell you that the three of us had a feeling there was something going on between the two of you, even before you left town."

"You did?" Hudson leaned forward, his face brooding.

"You didn't hide it all that well," Garrison commented with a smile.

"Yeah. You're still not. It's disgusting." Flint shook his head. "Every time you're together, you look like you can't wait to pounce on each other. Makes me wanna puke butterflies and rainbows."

Leona blinked. Was this some sort of nightmare? It didn't make sense. "But if you knew..." she began helplessly.

"We did, or at least we had a damn good hunch. That's why, as soon as you left, we decided that we'd have to make a special exception. I mean, fate is fate, after all."

Hudson threw back his head and laughed, then launched himself out of his chair to slap Drake on the arm. "You really had me going there, you bastard!"

"Sorry, but you know I couldn't just let that go without giving you *some* sort of hell."

"If it were me, I would've stretched out the torture a lot longer," Flint added, grinning.

"So, now that we've covered that and considering I've got a plane to catch, this meeting is adjourned."

Leona left the conference room with emotions swirling around her head. She knew this meant they could both keep their jobs, but she didn't quite know how Hudson was feeling. It was strange to realize just how much weight she was now giving to someone else's thoughts and emotions instead of just her own.

She and Hudson were the last to leave the conference room, and as the rest of them made their way to the garage, she headed toward the door at the front of the building. But Hudson wrapped his arm around her waist and pulled her close. "Can I give you a ride?"

She looked up at him, noting the passion in his

eyes. "I don't quite know where I'm going," she admitted. There hadn't been much time to think about it, and the last thing she wanted to do was return to Tracy's apartment.

"How about my place?" He turned her around, keeping his grip on her as they headed for the garage.

She giggled, feeling like a teenager. Or maybe, more like how she imagined teenagers felt when they were with someone they were crazy about. She liked the way Hudson's strong arm felt around her waist, and she liked how he was possessive of her, even when it was annoying. "Sounds like a plan."

"You know, you didn't have to stick up for me back there." He opened the passenger door and let her in, coming around to the driver's seat.

"Sure I did. It made sense for me to get fired; I'm new. But I never imagined they'd let both of us go, or at least try to make us think that way." At the time, she'd been so pissed off at their little joke, but knowing it was all in good fun, she could laugh about it now.

"Maybe I was going to stick up for you and let you keep the job instead of me. I mean, I've still got my company." He pulled out of the garage and slid the windows down. The evening was cool for the season, and the setting sun threw a pink and purple backdrop behind the skyline.

"Don't you think you've already done me enough favors?" she asked. "I mean, I saw what happened back there at the clubhouse. You killed for me."

His knuckles tightened on the steering wheel at the memory. "And I'd do it again. I couldn't stand the thought of someone hurting you. But that doesn't mean I've done you enough favors. I'm definitely not done."

By the time they reached his apartment building and rode the private elevator to the penthouse, Leona could feel the desire rolling off of him. It met her own and continued to build. As soon as they stepped into the living room, he had his arms around her. Leona melted as his lips pressed against hers, demanding, exploring, his tongue like electric velvet as it slipped against hers. His hands promised to fulfill her every desire as they roved over her, pulling at the clothes that had felt like simple necessities until they became a barrier that kept their skin from touching.

Her own body surged with need. She knew exactly what he was capable of, and she trembled merely at the thought. Her blood sizzled in her veins as she let him bring her through the living room and to the master bedroom, a massive affair with a bed so high, he had to lift her onto it.

"Leona," he breathed as he slid his hands inside the waistband of her jeans, cupping her backside as he used his forearms to push away the denim.

She was breathless to the point of being light-headed, and when he kissed her between the legs and she felt his heated tongue through the silk of her panties, she thought she might pass out. Her back arched as he moved the material aside and caressed her soft folds with his tongue. "Yes?"

"I want you to stay here with me." Hudson stopped his ministrations only long enough to remove the rest of her clothing, his hands running in luxurious and appreciative lines up and down her body before bringing his mouth back to her core. "I want you to be here every night."

She braced one foot on his broad shoulder as she clutched at the sheets. They'd hardly been in the door a minute and he was already working her into a frenzy, but she wasn't complaining. "You do?"

"God, yes." He proved it with his efforts, using the body of his tongue and alternating it with the tip to bring her into a turmoil. "I've got you now, and I don't want to ever let you go."

Leona's thighs clenched around his neck as her

abdominal muscles grew taut and the inside of her body broke into heated waves that rushed through her body. His words were turning her on as much as his actions. "Then don't," she panted. "Don't ever let me go."

"Anything you say." Hudson brought his body over hers, hovering over her.

Leona bit her lip as she studied him. He was pure perfection and she knew just how gorgeous he was in his other form as well. She'd never be tired of looking at him, and definitely never tired of touching him. Her hands spread across his chest, down his rippling stomach and to the arousal that waited for her. She wrapped her fingers around it, feeling the desire welling inside her once again.

"I love you," he whispered, leaning forward so that his mouth was near her ear. His kissed the top of her neck just below her lobe, sending a shiver down her spine. "Like I've never loved anyone else in my entire life."

She kissed him then as she wrapped her legs around him, demanding that he plunge inside her where he belonged. Her nerves were alive with wonder as they moved like a symphony, fitting so perfectly together. She felt as though she could never get enough of him, like every time was still something new. Leona commanded him at the same time that she surrendered to him, and she felt them climbing higher together until they both fell over the edge.

Her muscles relaxed as they lay together afterward, and Hudson trailed his fingers languidly over her skin. They didn't need to speak. They simply knew that this was right. She kicked herself for ever thinking she could give this up.

14

Hudson sat at the desk in his office, working away. He'd hired the country's top scientists and technology masterminds to work for Taylor Communications, but he knew he'd always want to get involved in the work himself. He wasn't the type of CEO to just sit back and let everyone else do the work while he got the credit for it. Besides, there was always plenty to do.

But today, he felt himself getting distracted. He could get easily lost in algorithms and coding, but his mind constantly wandered to something else he'd rather be doing. He sighed and pushed himself back from the desk, picking up his phone and dialing the number at the top of his list.

Leona picked up after several rings, sounding

excited. "Hey! How did you know I was thinking about you?"

"Just hoping, I guess." He smiled naturally simply at hearing her voice. "I just wanted to see how you were doing."

"You're not sick of me yet?" she teased.

They lived together in his apartment, which had made Hudson realize just how empty it'd been before she'd come along. They worked together on the SOS Force, of course, so they saw each other plenty. But he couldn't get enough of her. "Never."

"Well, I'm really glad you called." The exhilaration in her voice was coming through even more now, and Hudson could tell that she was barely containing herself. "I was going to tell you in person, but I can't wait. You know how I said I wanted something to do in between missions?"

The two of them had talked quite a bit about that, actually. Leona felt edgy and bored when Hudson was at work and wanted to find a satisfying way to spend her time. "I do."

"Well, I found something that should work perfectly. I'm going to volunteer for Habitat for Humanity right here in D.C. They need people to build homes for veterans. I couldn't resist!"

Hudson felt warm and calm when speaking to

her, and genuinely happy. He knew she needed something to keep her busy and make her feel useful, and he understood that. It was the same thing he needed from his own life, and he wanted nothing more than for her to be happy. "That's wonderful, baby."

"I know! I looked at some other opportunities, but they were going to be much longer commitments out of the country, ones that would keep me from really being on the Force. This way, I can serve both veterans and shifters. I don't think my life could get any better." She laughed happily.

"I know that feeling. Speaking of the Force, Drake called me a few minutes ago. He's got a mission that he says will be perfect for us. We're to go to HQ tonight to get all the details."

"I don't suppose we'll get to pose as suburban honeymooners again, will we? I'm sure in the mood for a block party and some of your cowboy caviar."

"I don't know yet," Hudson replied, "but I do know I can't wait to go on another mission with you. I'll see you then. I love you."

"I love you, too. Bye."

He hung up, looking at the phone for a long minute. Leona wasn't even in the same room with him, and yet he felt the most comforting sense of peace settling over him. He was about to head out on another mission with the woman of his dreams, a woman he knew he was bound to forever with the most fierce loyalty in the universe.

And he couldn't wait.

ABOUT THE AUTHOR

Meg Ripley is an author of steamy shifter romances. A Seattle native, Meg can often be found curled up in a local coffee house with her laptop.

FREE BOOK SERIES!

Download Meg's entire *Caught Between Dragons* series when you sign up for her newsletter!

Sign up by visiting Meg's Facebook page: https://www.facebook.com/authormegripley/